A Death in Utopia

Adele Fasick

MonganBooks
SAN FRANCISCO, CALIFORNIA

Book Layout ©2013 BookDesignTemplates.com

A Death in Utopia/ Adele Fasick. -- 1st ed.
ISBN 978-0-9853152-2-1

*Dedicated to Pamela, Laura and Julia,
my three Graces*

CHAPTER ONE

Charlotte's New Beginning

September 20, 1842

"Where are you going so early?" Ellen Geary peered sleepily at Charlotte who was dressing quietly in the chilly room. The sky outside the bedroom window was just turning from black to gray.

"Out to see the new piglets, if they've come. I want to take my class to see the newborns this morning. We've only one pig, so there aren't many chances."

"I'll come along with you." Ellen decided quickly.

The two of them soon slipped out the back door of the Hive, and walked across the dewy grass toward the barn. The milking group were gathering buckets and singing one of the familiar hymns they heard so often here:

The world is all a fleeting show

For Man's illusion given;

The smiles of joy, the tears of woe

Deceitful shine, deceitful flow

There's nothing true but heaven!

"They'll scare the pigs," grumbled Ellen. "What makes them so cheerful at this hour?"

"Why shouldn't they be cheerful?" Sometimes Ellen's grumbling surprised Charlotte. She hinted about mysterious troubles Charlotte had never suspected.

"Mr. Ripley didn't sound so cheerful when he was talking to Mr. Pratt and Mr. Dana in the parlor last night. They were talking about needing money to plant crops in the spring. Someone has to talk to a banker about getting another loan."

"Another loan?" Charlotte echoed. The business side of Brook Farm was a mystery to her. George and Sophia Ripley had organized the experimental community almost two years earlier and had gathered enough followers to make it a reality. Even though they called their community a farm, the Ripleys certainly were not farmers. Mr. Ripley was a benign man who looked like the minister he had been before resigning his pulpit to found the group. His wife, a tall, spare woman with graying hair and a long, anxious face, struggled to keep the laundry room going and to supervise the cooking.

The Ripleys had persuaded a number of their friends to become Association members and put money into the project. They all dreamed of a life that would balance intellectual efforts with manual labor. Their intellectual lives seemed to be flourishing; they certainly spent enough time arguing about life's higher goals and reading their poetry to one another. The labor part was not going quite as well—harvests had been bad for the two years since they started. No one in the group knew how to do practical things—only last week they had to ask a local farmer to show them how to mend harnesses and hoes so they could get through another season.

The day that had started cheerfully seemed to dim. Was it possible the Ripleys were in real trouble? Was it possible Brook Farm could fail? What would happen to all the grand plans for reforming the world then? And what if the school failed? Charlotte would have to find a new job in a more conventional school where she would endlessly teach the children to memorize Bible verses and pious maxims.

In the pig shed behind the barn, they found the sow and her piglets safely ensconced on a bed of hay. Mr. Platt, the neighboring farmer who often helped the inexperienced Brook Farmers, had watched over the birth. And Fred, a gangly fourteen-year-old student, was crouched beside him keeping an eye on the fragile piglets.

Charlotte was satisfied she would be able to take the children out to see the animals later. Leaving Ellen with Fred and Mr. Platt she walked on up the hillside to look for late blueberries. Even after six months living in Massachusetts, she was still not used to the New England weather. Autumn came with breathtaking suddenness. Brisk winds blew feathery seed pods across the fields and turned maple leaves into flashes of unnerving scarlet. Every morning the hillside flamed with new patches of red and yellow. This was nothing like the leisurely British autumns she was used to when mist rose gently from soggy, mossy fields. In the crisp air Charlotte was filled with energy and hope for the revolution being planned at Brook Farm no matter what Ellen said.

The sun was warm on her back as she scrambled through a broken place in the low stone wall behind the barn. Plump gray squirrels with acorns in their cheeks ran to get out of her way and a pair of blue jays squawked harshly from a pine tree.

Soon she reached the tiny stream and easily crossed it on a couple of rocks. The blueberry bushes looked rather bare and stripped of their berries. Someone else was looking for blueberries too. Abigail Pretlove, wearing a white dress and a bonnet trimmed with pink flowers, was pulling at the bushes to see whether any berries were left. It was easy to see she was a boarder and didn't have to share in the work of the farm. Who else would have worn a white dress on a weekday? A minute later her young son, Timothy, burst through the bushes and saw Charlotte.

"Good morning, Miss Edgerton," he cried. "See what I found." He held out his hand to show a blue-black beetle he had caught. Timothy was one of Charlotte's liveliest primary students. He smiled easily and was always showing her bugs and stones or asking her to sing a song for the class. His mother Abigail smiled a lot too, and all the men smiled back at her, even Mr. Ripley. She certainly was pretty. Charlotte sighed and thought of how her mother used to say to her, "If you don't have beauty, Charlotte, at least you have a happy heart and a clever head. You will have to make your own fortune in this world."

"There are very few berries left," Abigail called. "We can all share what I found. I'm afraid the berry season is over."

Abigail and Charlotte started walking back to the house. As they crossed the meadow they saw a tall man in a dark suit walking toward the main door of the Hive.

"That must be another minister from Boston come to talk to Mr. Ripley about his great experiment," Charlotte commented. She swerved across the lawn to welcome him. Abigail trailed after her, but hung back a few steps.

"Good morning. I'm Charlotte Edgerton," she called as she got closer. "Are you looking for Mr. Ripley?"

"Yes, indeed. I am Winslow Hopewell. Mr. Ripley invited me to visit for a few days, but where is everyone?"

His name was familiar. Winslow Hopewell was one of the best-known ministers in Boston. His church was filled every Sunday, especially, Charlotte had heard, with women who admired the handsome preacher. Handsome he certainly was. He wore his black hair longer than most men and his deep gray eyes and pale skin made him look intensely spiritual. He would be very pleasing to look at in the pulpit. Charlotte sighed. Why wasn't an attractive spiritual leader like Reverend Hopewell a member of the Brook Farm community trying to reform the world instead of living in comfort in Boston preaching to foolish women?

"The hour is early even for us," Charlotte answered. "But everyone will be at breakfast soon and I'm sure Mr. Ripley will be glad to see you."

She turned back to look at Abigail, who was several yards behind, bending over to look at a flower or something in the grass with Timothy. It didn't seem very hospitable. "Would you like to meet the Reverend Hopewell?"

Abigail straightened up and looked at them and as she did, Charlotte heard Mr. Hopewell draw his breath in sharply. "I believe we have met before," he finally said as Abigail approached. "Good morning, Miss Coffin."

"My name is Mrs. Pretlove now," Abigail answered. "This is my son, Timothy. It has been quite some time since we last met, Mr. Hopewell."

The minister stood silently for a minute searching Abigail's face but she turned her head aside to avoid his gaze. They had both forgotten Charlotte until she spoke. "You two must have much to talk about. I'll take Timothy to breakfast."

She took Timothy by the hand and as they walked toward the kitchen to drop off the blueberries she kept glancing back at Abigail Pretlove and the Reverend Hopewell talking together. He didn't seem to be in a great hurry to see Mr. Ripley.

Timothy tugged at her skirt. "Look at this pretty bug on the flower. Let's take it to the classroom and show it to the others." Charlotte let him search among the leaves looking for small creatures, but her eyes were on Abigail and Mr. Hopewell. He leaned over her, talking away as though he were giving a sermon. His long black shadow blotted out her white dress and darkened the meadow grass behind her.

CHAPTER TWO

Abigail Hears a Speaker

September 21, 1842

Abigail heard a buzz of talk as she walked downstairs and into the large parlor where the famous guest would speak. People had been talking for days about Lydia Maria Child. She infuriated many people by speaking out on the most outrageous topics. Her book advocating the immediate freeing of all slaves in the Southern states was so explosive the Boston Athenaeum took away her library privileges. She was just the type of speaker Brook Farmers prided themselves on inviting to visit their community. Scaring the local farmers with visions of radical social changes was part of their plan to change the world.

That evening almost everyone at the Farm crowded into the parlor to listen to the talk. Fanny Gray, Mrs. Ripley's best friend, had taken the younger children into a side room and was keeping them entertained with stories and music while the adults listened to the speaker. Abigail could hear Fanny's voice leading the children in singing "Oh Canaan, bright Canaan" and she smiled when she heard Timothy's high-pitched voice raised to ask a question. Despite her pride in his searching questions, it was nice to have someone else responsible for answering them for a few hours.

The bare room had very little furniture except for the wooden ladder-back chairs around the walls. The older people sat on these, making a circle of figures in sober dark blue or brown clothes. Abigail knew her white dress made her stand out, but she loved that dress and felt pretty in it although she sometimes wondered whether her stern Quaker father would approve. Ten years in New England had made a difference. She wasn't the mousey girl in gray she had been in Philadelphia before her parents died. Eight years of being a mother to Timothy changed her too; she was much stronger than the timid girl Winslow Hopewell used to know. He was sitting now at the front of the room with the Ripleys and Mrs. Child and looking around at everyone, but avoiding her eyes.

Most of the young people sat on the bare floor. Almost all of the students from the Brook Farm school were there. Red-headed Fred was sitting as close as he could get to the speaker. And beside him was his shadow, clumsy, dark-haired Lloyd gazing around the room with his muddy gray eyes. A few outsiders crowded around the doorway. Abigail recognized Mr. Platt. With him was a younger man who looked enough like him to be his brother. There was also a tall colored woman standing just outside the door pulling a gray shawl around her broad shoulders.

Mrs. Child was seated in a high backed chair at the front of the room. She was forty years old at least, but she still looked elegant in a quiet dark gray dress with a filmy white collar. There was no gray in her dark hair and when she spoke, her clear voice reached everyone in the room.

"I am going to talk tonight about an unpopular subject. We who live in New England speak harshly of slaveholders in the Southern States, but we must not congratulate ourselves. Thanks to our soil and climate, and the early influence of the Quakers, the form of slavery does not exist among us; but the very spirit of the hateful and mischievous thing is here in all its strength."

Abigail heard a scuffle of feet at the back of the room and someone coughed. Mr. Platt scowled at the speaker.

"An unjust law exists in this Commonwealth, by which marriages between persons of different color is pronounced illegal." Mrs. Child continued. Mrs. Ripley, seated at the front of the room with her husband showed no sign of being shocked; her face was perfectly still as she listened. "I am aware of the ridicule to which I may subject myself by alluding to this, but I have lived too long, and observed too much, to be disturbed by the world's mockery. The government ought not to be invested with power to control the affections, any more than the consciences of citizens. A man has at least as good a right to choose his wife, as he has to choose his religion."

That was too much for Mr. Platt. He spluttered out, "You people have no right to come here with your wild ideas about how we should live. Everybody knows whites and blacks don't belong together. That's why God made 'em different. It's only radicals and Quakers want them to live together."

Abigail looked at Winslow Hopewell, who was leaning forward in his chair, his attention focused on Mrs. Child. He paid no attention to the outburst. Very different from her father who always jumped into the middle of a fight if his beliefs were being questioned. Impulsively she stood up and spoke.

"We Quakers believe all human beings should live together in peace. A man's character isn't shown in the color of his skin."

"Hurrah for the Quakers!" one of the students blurted out abruptly. Mr. Ripley clapped his hands and told everyone to quiet down.

"This is no way to treat our guest," he said sharply. "We will listen to what Mrs. Child has to say and then we can ask questions. But there must be no more interruptions."

The room became quiet, but again Abigail heard a rustle of movement in back of her and a few more coughs as the Platts settled down. She wondered why they had come. She doubted that tonight's talk was giving the visitors a better feeling about Brook Farmers.

Mrs. Child went on to talk about how quarrels between abolitionists were threatening the efforts to end slavery. "Whether we believe that slaves should be freed immediately to live among us, or believe that freed slaves should find a homeland in another country, we must work together. Remember there are still many Americans who have met violent ends because they advocated ending slavery. Only five years ago Elijah Lovejoy was killed and his press destroyed because he published an anti-slavery newspaper. And the U.S. Postmaster General has proclaimed that the post offices will refuse to deliver anti-slavery literature."

The students sitting on the floor stirred restlessly and Fred ran his fingers impatiently through his red hair. Mrs. Child must have felt the tension too because she soon ended her talk.

George Ripley announced there was time for questions and Fred was the first to jump up. "What can we do here at Brook Farm?" he asked. "Why don't we have any members who are former slaves?"

George Ripley exchanged an exasperated glance with his wife, but fended off Fred's question by announcing, "Our distinguished guest the Reverend Hopewell might like to start the discussion."

Winslow Hopewell smiled faintly at the Ripleys and turned to ask Mrs. Child about her work as editor of the National Anti-Slavery Standard. "We admire your courage in continuing to write about this vexing, and sometimes dangerous issue." he said. "I am sure we all hope the journal will soon reach a large audience."

Fred scowled sulkily at his shoes, but no one spoke as Mrs. Child mentioned a few articles that had appeared in her journal. At the back of the room the colored woman pulled her shawl close around her and slipped out the door. Mrs. Child raised her head and looked after the retreating figure; she leaned forward as though to speak again, but sank back in her chair as George Ripley stood up and announced the meeting was over.

Most of the audience started to leave, but a few lingered and moved toward the front to talk with Mrs. Child. Fred repeated his question, and Mrs. Child said firmly that she had strongly urged the Community to accept some freedmen as members.

"It's difficult enough to get any members," George Ripley explained. "Some of these reforms will just have to wait."

"Perhaps it is more important for people here to understand themselves and try to cultivate their own values before they turn to reforming society," added Winslow. His voice was deeper than Abigail remembered it and he sounded a little smug, just like many other ministers.

The smugness bothered her and she forced herself to speak up again. "Most people don't want to be reformed. Even some of the

Quaker meetings have had trouble when they try to introduce freedmen into their groups."

That caught Mr. Platt's attention and he agreed heartily. "People like to live with others of their kind," he insisted in his rough voice. "Mixing the races together brings nothing but trouble. I mean no offense to the lady, but folks here don't want to be told what they should do and outsiders should watch what they say." With that he turned and stomped out of the room.

"That's enough discussion for tonight," said Mr. Ripley. "Our guest is tired, I am sure."

The students reluctantly edged toward the door and Abigail followed them. Winslow still hadn't acknowledged her, but now he walked over to hold the door open and as she passed, he handed her a small, white envelope and said. "I hope you will consider this."

CHAPTER THREE

Charlotte Sees Too Much

September 23, 1842.

When Charlotte got back to her room, she was too excited to go straight to bed. Imagine hearing Lydia Maria Child in person. Her books were read everywhere and people flocked to hear her speak. She was even more impressive in person than in her books. How did she find the courage to speak out so confidently on topics no one else mentioned?

Would Charlotte ever be able to do as much? Sighing and leaning on the windowsill looking out on the grassy lawns she watched the full moon casting long shadows of the trees. An owl hooted in the distance and somewhere a dog barked. A patch of white at the edge of the trees behind the Eyrie caught Charlotte's eye. Was one of the cows out? Or was it a clump of Queen Anne's lace blowing in the wind?

Just then she saw a something bright—a flash of light near the barn. Only a flicker at first and then she realized it was a lantern. Why was someone down there with a lantern? Who could that be?

She leaned as far out the window as she dared and tried to see who it was.

She saw the flash of white again—there were two people out by the barn. And one of them was Abigail. It was Abigail in her white dress standing with someone who was carrying a lantern. Someone tall who moved closer to her as he lifted the lantern. The light caught Abigail's face looking up and, sure enough, it was Winslow Hopewell who was leaning toward her and talking. That was a surprise. Hadn't Abigail said they hadn't seen each other in years? Were they trying to make up for lost time? That sounded romantic, but why they were meeting secretly so late at night?

The next day Mrs. Child went back to Boston and on to wherever else she was giving talks that month. Charlotte longed for a chance to talk with her, but teaching the primary children kept her occupied all day. When she finally dismissed them, Mrs. Child was gone.

For the next two weeks life continued to seem normal in the Community. Winslow Hopewell stayed on longer than expected. He and Mr. Ripley spent hours in the study with papers spread out on the desk in front of them. Charlotte caught glimpses of them frowning as they walked on the grounds deep in conversation. Were they talking about serious issues in religion and philosophy or were they more worried about money and how good the harvest would be?

Most of Charlotte's days were filled with routine chores. In the classroom she struggled to keep her primary students interested in reading their primers. Timothy and the others loved the little jingles in the book, but she soon got tired of simple-minded verses.

> I like to see a lit-tle dog,
>
> And pat him on the head;

> So pret-ti-ly he wags his tail
> When-ev-er he is fed.

She tried making up verses of her own

> Whene'er you see a pretty mouse
> A nibbling at the cheese,
> Don't pull its tail or tweak its ear
> Just ask it to say 'Please'.

> For all small animals are our friends
> And we should treat them well.
> Boys and girls who torment them
> May find themselves in Hell.

Of course she never wrote these out for the students. Mrs. Ripley might send her back to England if she had dared, but sometimes she recited them to Ellen at night. The two of them tried to outdo each other in creating teasing verses. Even though they both believed in what the Ripleys were doing—what all of them were doing—it was hard to be as solemn about it as some of the older members were.

Sometimes when her class was restless, Charlotte took them outside to sit on the grass under one of the oak trees for their lesson. Even though it was almost the end of September, the sun was still warm and goldenrod still lined the road. One afternoon when she had taken the class out there and was reading Aesop's fable about the jay and the peacocks, they were interrupted by a fat blue jay that swooped down and landed right at her feet. He was probably only looking for acorns, but it seemed as though he was objecting to being made a fool of by the peacocks like the jay in their story. The children laughed and clapped. Charlotte looked up and saw Winslow Hopewell and Abigail Pretlove walking across the lawn. She had often noticed them talking to each other and wondered whether he had lingered on at the Farm because of Abigail. Which one of them was the jay trying to impress the other?

Whether or not they were flirting they didn't have much time by themselves. Mr. Ripley and Mr. Dana walked past the tree where Charlotte was sitting with the children and headed straight for the couple. Mr. Ripley's gentle face was twisted into a scowl and she heard him say as they stalked by, "...doesn't realize how serious this is. We all need to pull together to make..." That was all she heard, but she saw them stop to talk to Hopewell. Then the three men moved back toward the house.

Soon it was time for the children's music lesson, so Charlotte took the group back into the Hive and looked around for Fanny Gray. They taught music together. Fanny had a lovely voice, and Charlotte could beat time and lead the children in responding. Ellen sometimes joined them too and taught ballads she had learned as a child in Ireland. There was no sign of Fanny so Ellen and Charlotte started the lesson. They wanted the children to learn the words to a new song to sing it in the dining room on Sunday when Mrs. Ripley liked to have some entertainment from the school children.

> I had a little nut tree
> Nothing would it bear
> But a silver nutmeg and a golden pear.
> The King of Spain's daughter
> Came to visit me
> And all for the sake of my little nut tree.

Everyone was having fun singing and talking about pears and how good they tasted when Fanny Gray came in looking very serious.

"Do you think we should let the children sing about kings?" she asked. "We're all good Americans who don't believe in kings. Don't you know any better songs?"

Ellen quickly started singing

> Ye fair maids of London, who lead a single life
> I'd sooner be a barrow girl than a rich merchant's wife,
> For so early in the morning you hear me to cry,
> Artichokes and cauliflowers, pretty maids will you buy?

"That's a cheerful song," Charlotte said, "and it's not about a king or his daughter. A barrow girl sounds more like someone who should join Brook Farm. We need someone who could sell the crops we raise and make some money for us."

"We certainly need people to join us," Fanny muttered. "Too many people are leaving and outsiders who say they support us just slither away without doing a thing. Why don't they understand that the kind of community we are building is going to change the whole country?"

Charlotte wanted to ask what she meant about people leaving, but the children were growing restless so she took them to dinner.

As September turned into October, the wind became brisk. Mornings were chillier and darker clouds scudded across the sky. The tiny piglets in the barn were growing livelier and the last of the scarlet maple leaves were drifting down and littering the grass. Charlotte pulled a shawl tight around her shoulders each morning as she walked across the lawn toward the Hive to start working with the kitchen group.

The sharp sound of a slamming door startled her one morning and she was even more surprised to see Mrs. Ripley hurrying across the grass toward the clump of trees behind the barn. Then Charlotte noticed a group of people on the hillside and she heard faint voices. She quickly followed the sounds.

Abigail Pretlove was standing stiffly twisting her hands in her shawl; her white dress bright against the dark pine trees. Her cheeks were streaked with tears and she was crying incoherently and trying to talk, although Charlotte couldn't make out any words. Mr. Ripley, Fanny, and some of the students were there. Everyone was silent, looking intently at something on the ground.

Mrs. Ripley went to Abigail, put her arm around her, and began to lead her down the hill toward the Hive. Abigail stumbled uncertainly as though she didn't know where she was walking.

As Charlotte moved closer to the group, she saw the dark form of a man on the grass. She gasped as she realized it was. Winslow Homer, lay on his back his arm flung out and with a trickle of blood on his forehead. Mr. Ripley was leaning over him, but he straightened up as he heard more people coming up the hill.

He spoke to Charles Dana and the two other men who were there. "I am afraid there is no hope for him. He is dead. We must get the women back to the house and then we can carry the Reverend Hopewell in."

Charlotte, Fanny and Mrs. Geary walked silently back to the Hive. Ellen was in the kitchen and Charlotte muttered a few words about what had happened. No one was able to talk much. The scene on the hillside was too dreadful to think about but they knew they would never forget it.

Nothing was normal that day, and Charlotte was not surprised when Mrs. Ripley decided to cancel all the regular classes and let the children play quietly in the parlor. Charlotte walked back to her room as soon as she could. She needed time to be quiet and think about what had happened. None of it made any sense.

Had the Reverend Hopewell stumbled and fallen on the ground? But why was there blood on his forehead? Had he met someone on the hillside and quarreled with him? It was hard to believe a respectable minister would get into a fight that would lead to such violence. But why would anyone try to injure him?

Her thoughts were interrupted when Ellen slipped into the room. She reported that the men had carried Reverend Hopewell's body back to the Hive and laid it out in George Ripley's study.

"This terrible death reminds me about what Mrs. Child said when she spoke here. Remember she told us that people wouldn't let us live in peace because too many people at Brook Farm favor abolition?" Ellen commented.

Charlotte walked restlessly around their small room. "I wonder what Mrs. Child would say about this. Perhaps she knows of people around here who might attack someone they suspected of abolitionist sentiment."

"Is Mrs. Child still in Boston?" asked Ellen.

"I don't know. But you know what we can do? We could go and ask at Miss Peabody's bookstore. She knows everyone who is lecturing in the area. Perhaps she can tell us where Mrs. Child is," Charlotte answered eagerly.

"We can ride in Mr. Gerritson's wagon," Ellen added. "Mr. Ripley has asked him to notify the Sheriff. He'll be driving to the city soon. There is nothing we can do here."

Charlotte was relieved to have something active to do. She snatched up her shawl and bonnet and the two of them ran down to catch Mr. Gerritson's wagon before he left. .

CHAPTER FOUR

Daniel's Rainy Day in Boston

October 10, 1842.

An early morning rain had made the streets wet; fallen leaves and blobs of horse dung turned the pavement into a treacherous slide as Daniel Gallagher hurried to reach the newspaper office before anyone else. Already this morning he had made his rounds of the fish market and the stagecoach yard looking for any trace of news. Didn't anything exciting ever happen in Boston? He needed a good story to persuade Mr. Cabot to give him a job. He knew he could do it if he was given a chance. And he swore he wouldn't end up working as a laborer on the docks like so many other Irish immigrants. All he needed was one chance and he could make his mother proud—make some money too so he could bring her over to America.

This morning he felt he was getting lucky. A mystery in that strange community out in West Roxbury? How did one of those radicals get himself killed? Glory be to God what a stroke of luck if he could get that story!

He was almost running now, hoping to reach the editor's office before one of those slick Boston reporters got there and grabbed his chance. He'd heard the story from an Irishman, Rory his name was, who'd been out on the road early coming back to the city after sleeping in some farmer's barn all night. A lot of the new immigrants do that. When you're just off the boat and not a penny to your name, you'll sleep anywhere. He was slipping through a patch of woods so as not to be seen, when he noticed a group of people huddled around something on the ground and looking scared silly. Rory managed to get close enough to hear them talking about someone being dead and then he skedaddled out of there so they wouldn't think he had anything to do with it. When Daniel ran into him at the edge of the Common, he was white as a ghost and glad enough to tell the story when he was offered a couple of currant buns.

Daniel hurried down Tremont Street to Mr. Cabot's office and arrived at the steps just as Mr. Cabot was approaching from the other direction. "Mr. Cabot, sir," Daniel began. "I have just heard there has been a terrible accident this morning out at Brook Farm. Someone is dead. With your permission I would like to write the story for the *Transcript.*"

"Hmm...What do you know about Brook Farm? An Irishman like you has no idea of who those people are or what they are doing. And how did you hear of this mysterious death? Was this a brawl between some drunken Paddys?"

"No, but it was an Irishman who told me. He was just passing by and heard the news. Readers of the *Transcript* would be interested in what's happening at Reverend Ripley's Farm. I can walk out there this morning and get the news for you before the other newspapers have heard what happened."

"All right then, go do it, but you had better stop at Miss Peabody's bookstore first and find out more about those people and what they are up to. Then you'll be able to ask sensible questions."

Daniel knew about Brook Farm already. His Aunt Maggie was a cook there and his cousin Ellen was going to their school. Still, he didn't want to offend Mr. Cabot, so he decided to stop at the bookstore before starting out. He could take a look at some of the books this George Ripley had written. Could Ripley have been the man who was killed?

Stooping under the low doorway, Daniel went into the dim bookstore; the towering bookshelves covering every wall always made him greedy to read. There was no sign of Miss Peabody, so he started looking at the shelves to see what he could find.

A few minutes later, the door into the back room of the shop opened and Miss Peabody came in with two young women. His cousin Ellen! What was she doing here? He didn't recognize her friend who was talking excitedly in a low voice as if she were urging Ellen to do something. A lock of dark hair was slipping out of her bonnet and the set of her jaw made him willing to bet she would win any argument she was in.

Miss Peabody came toward Daniel, her large body blocking his view of the girls. Her frizzy white hair was escaping from her cap in all directions, but her welcoming smile was good to see.

"I need to find out more about Brook Farm out in West Roxbury. Do you have any books about George Ripley?"

Before he had finished speaking, Ellen broke in. "What are you doing here, Daniel?" she asked. "And why do you want to know about Brook Farm? I thought you said you wouldn't waste your time on foolish schemes to change the world."

The second girl frowned at Daniel when Ellen said that, her dark eyes taking in his shabby suit so intently he was sure she could see spilled currants from his breakfast buns. He tried not to look at her while he answered Ellen.

"Did you just come from there? Do you know anything about someone getting killed? I'm going to write a story about it for the newspaper."

"We don't need any newspapers interfering," said Ellen's friend sharply in a fancy English voice. Turning to Ellen she added, "We can't talk to outsiders about what happened."

Ellen introduced them, but even after hearing he was Ellen's cousin and could be trusted, Charlotte Edgerton didn't look any friendlier. But Daniel knew he would learn more about Brook Farm from them than from any book, so he walked out of the shop with them.

"Mr. Cabot told me to talk to Miss Peabody," Daniel explained, "to find out more about Brook Farm. She knows most of what is going on all over the city, but I am sure you know more about Brook Farm."

"That we do," said Ellen. "We were hoping to find Lydia Maria Child and ask her some questions, but Miss Peabody told us she is on her way to Ohio to visit relatives."

Charlotte Edgerton looked at Daniel. "Why are you so curious about what happened? Are you hoping to write a story to discredit Brook Farm?"

"Not at all, Miss Edgerton. I want to discover the truth of what happened. Surely that will not discredit your community."

Ellen broke in quickly. "Come to Aunt Bridget's with us. We can tell you what happened. Jonas Gerritson is going to pick us up in his wagon and give us a ride back to the Farm. If you go with us you'll be there faster than walking."

They turned down a narrow, muddy street where a group of children gathered around a puddle were kicking water at each other. A red faced man sat on the steps of one house muttering to himself and singing snatches of songs. He stared at the girls as they walked past and called out, "Oh, you pretty girlies, won't you stop and talk with me a while?"

Daniel could feel his cheeks flushing as he realized what this must look like to the Englishwoman. An excuse for her to think that all the Irish were drunken fools. They were worse than Americans when it came to looking down on the Irish. Bringing her along to visit Aunt Bridget would never have been his idea.

They climbed the narrow staircase, and entered a long, high ceilinged room left over from when the house had been a mansion. Now the room was bare with no carpet on the floor. The only chairs were straight backed wooden ones drawn up around a large table littered with fabric. The walls were painted a light green, but the paint was dirty and peeling, with blotches of moisture stains from a leaky roof. A large crucifix on a table against the wall was the only ornament. At the base of the crucifix a tiny stump of a candle set in a cracked cup flickered weakly. Another reason for Miss Edgerton to laugh at the "superstitious nonsense!" of the Irish.

Aunt Bridget was even thinner than she had been last time Daniel had seen her, but her curly black hair and blue eyes still made her look young. She was sitting at the table sewing a fancy hat. Ellen introduced Charlotte to her and asked if they could stay for an hour or so while waiting for Jonas Gerritson.

"Sure, I'm pleased to meet you. You'll not mind if I keep sewing while we talk. Mrs. Perkins will have a conniption if I don't finish this bonnet today. The house is quiet as a tomb. Theresa's off asking about a job as a nursemaid that she heard about. And Maureen is working with Mrs. Daly doing starching today. Brian is off some-where. I never know where that scamp is."

Daniel told all of them what he had heard from Rory that morn-ing. It wasn't much that he knew. He needed to find out more about what had happened and who had been killed.

"Oh, he'll get into trouble for talking about a killing," murmured Aunt Bridget. "They'll accuse him of murder like as not."

Both Ellen and Charlotte looked troubled when she said that. "We don't know what happened. Don't talk about murder. Winslow Hopewell was a famous man and a well-known minister. Why would anyone harm him?"

"Winslow Hopewell?" Daniel knew he was the minister at one of the biggest Unitarian Churches in the city. "He wasn't a member of the Brook Farm Community was he?"

"No, he was visiting Mr. Ripley," Charlotte answered. "He had been staying there for a few weeks. He stayed longer than most visi-tors, but I don't know that he was thinking of joining the Communi-ty."

Daniel was getting fidgety when the girls finally decided it was time to leave to meet Jonas Gerritson. Soon they were on their way, sitting in the back of the wagon along with sacks of onions and flour. The wagon moved slowly through the streets around the market, crowded as they were with wagons carrying food and crates of chickens, but before very long they were out on on a country road.

The rain had stopped and the meadows smelled sweet, not like the dung-splattered streets in Boston.

"Can you tell me more about what happened?" Daniel asked.

"It was all so fast," Charlotte Edgerton said. "I was on my way to the henhouse to see whether there were any fresh eggs" she paused and looked down at her lap. "And then I saw a commotion up by the pine trees. A minute later Mrs. Ripley came toward me with her arm around Abigail Pretlove, who looked as white as a ghost. Mrs. Ripley shook her head at me, so I knew I shouldn't say anything to them. I just ran over to the patch of trees. The men were looking at something dark on the ground.

At first I couldn't tell what it was—it was still pretty dark—and then I realized someone was lying on the ground. He seemed to be sleeping but when I walked toward him, I could see something was wrong. It was horrible! He had a big cut in his forehead and the blood had oozed down into his eyes. I couldn't look at him."

"I was in the kitchen," added Ellen. "As soon as Charlotte came bursting in, I started over there to see what had happened, but Mr. Ripley made all the women go back to the house. He said the men would take care of it. They were standing around and talking, but I couldn't see much from where I was."

"Mr. Ripley was trying to keep everyone calm. But Charlotte and I couldn't just sit there and wait for the sheriff to come. We decided to try to find Mrs. Child and see whether she knew if there were any anti-abolitionist troublemakers around this area. Besides, Mr. Ripley didn't want us to talk to the sheriff or tell anyone about what had happened. "

"He thinks we're silly, gossiping girls," Charlotte frowned scornfully as she spoke. "As if we'd tell secrets! And it was you, Mr. Gallagher, who told Miss Peabody about it. I don't think we should let this go into the newspapers."

"There's no way to keep it out, Miss Edgerton. Brook Farm has attracted a lot of attention and people want to know what is happening there. I'll write the truth and that's better than letting a lot of false rumors about crazy radicals spread throughout the city."

Charlotte still looked skeptical, but by this time the wagon was turning into the narrow lane leading to Brook Farm. As Mr. Gerritson pulled his horses to a halt in front of the barn, a tall red-haired boy in a floppy blue tunic ran out of the house and across to the wagon.

"It's a good thing you're back," he said, speaking to the girls. "We know who killed Winslow Hopewell. Mr. Platt figured it out. The sheriff is on his way now."

CHAPTER FIVE

Charlotte Searches for Answers

October 10, 1842

Charlotte gasped. This was what she had been afraid of. She didn't want to hear the words. She had been half-hoping it would turn out that somehow Reverend Hopewell had fallen and hit his head. She just couldn't believe—didn't want to believe—that anyone had deliberately done something so horrible. Brook Farm had been her haven from the tumult of life in England. Here she felt safe among friends. Now it had become a dangerous spot where bad things could happen. Was anyplace ever safe?

Daniel Gallagher jumped down from the wagon and stood in front of Fred, "How did Mr. Platt figure it out? How can he be sure? Who was it? What's his name? And why did he do it?" Daniel was half a head shorter than Fred and quite a bit thinner even though he must have been at least five years older. His black hair flopped across his pale forehead and his blue eyes peered intently at Fred.

"Who are you?" asked Fred, scowling a bit. "What are you doing here?" He stared at Daniel suspiciously, taking in his dark city suit, thin blue cravat, and the pencil poking out of his jacket pocket. Before Daniel could answer, Mr. Ripley came out of the Hive and walked over to the wagon.

"Are you a reporter, young man?" he asked Daniel. "We have no reason to speak to the newspapers about this. We don't want any scandal being spread. We'll take care of it ourselves. The sheriff is on his way."

"Sure the newspapers will find out, sir," protested Daniel. His brogue gave away his background, but his voice was respectful and polite. "If you tell me the details, I'll give them the straight story. You won't want wild rumors flying around."

Mr. Ripley looked at him seriously for a minute and then said, "Perhaps you are right, young man. Come with me. We can talk in my office." The two of them walked across the grass and into the building.

"You tell us about it, Fred," commanded Ellen. "Why does Mr. Platt think he knows what happened to Reverend Hopewell?" She and Charlotte headed toward the kitchen with Fred while Jonas Gerritson drove the wagon toward the barn. The grass was wet and squishy and the girls had to lift their skirts as high as they decently could to keep from getting muddy.

"Mr. Platt said he saw someone sneaking past his barn early this morning. Looked like he was just a tramp who'd slept there. Platt yelled after him and started to chase him, but the cows were hollering, so he figured he'd better do the milking. He just forgot about the man. It wasn't until he heard about poor Mr. Hopewell that he put two and two together. Who else would it be?"

"But there's no way to know for sure," Ellen broke in. "Mr. Platt didn't see what happened, did he?"

"He doesn't have to see it," Fred insisted. "It just makes sense. Don't you think so, Charlotte?"

Charlotte didn't know what to think. She had seen lots of tramps walking the roads in England and everyone was quick to accuse them whenever anything bad happened. Trouble was, anyone who was down on his luck could look like a tramp. One time her father picked up some apples that had fallen over a farmer's hedge and onto the road. Next thing he knew, the farmer was yelling and accusing him of stealing fruit from his orchard. Lucky for him the landlord was driving by and set things straight or else he might have had the sheriff after him.

By this time they were in the kitchen sitting at the large wooden table. Mrs. Ripley poked her head in from the laundry room "Charlotte, where have you been all this time? You had better gather up your primary class. Fanny has been tending them all morning. Everything is upset. Some of the children are crying. We need to get them back on their regular schedule. And Fred and Ellen, aren't you supposed to be in class? Mr. Dana's German class? I hope he hasn't forgotten. Where have you been? Nothing is going right. We want to keep everything as normal as possible."

Mrs. Ripley was wringing her hands and looking harried, not at all like her usual serene self. She didn't wait for an answer. Charlotte hurried off to take her charges to the school room and started listening to them recite their lesson for the day.

In the hallway she saw Daniel Gallagher coming out of Mr. Ripley's office. "Are you going to write all of this up for your newspaper?" she asked rather more sharply than she meant to.

"I'm going to try to find out the truth," he answered, frowning. "The man Mr. Platt saw must have been the fellow I met in Boston—

Rory O'Connor his name was. He didn't look or talk like a killer. He's poor and ignorant. They may lock him up before he knows what's happening to him. I'm going to track him down and see what he has to say."

"Why do you want to get mixed up in our troubles?" Charlotte was a little suspicious of how quickly Daniel Gallagher had taken on the job for himself.

"This is my chance," Daniel explained eagerly. "No one will ever give me a newspaper job unless I prove I can find a spectacular story and write it up faster than anyone else." He looked defiant as he added, "These rich Harvard boys think they're the only ones who can be newspapermen, but I'll show them. Besides, I don't like the way they decided Rory was guilty before they even talked to him."

Charlotte thought about her father and how quick people were to make accusations about people who looked shabby. Was that what Mr. Platt was doing? He didn't approve of Brook Farmers and all their radical ideas. He probably didn't approve of immigrants either, or anyone who looked like a tramp. She made up her mind to try to find the truth.

"Well, I'm going to look around here and ask some questions too." she said impulsively and then wondered whether she should get involved with this young reporter. But it was too late to change her mind. "Maybe between us we can figure out what happened."

Daniel looked at her uncertainly, but then he gave her quick, shy smile and said, "Perhaps we can work together. Stranger things have happened. At least we can try."

Later, as she listened to the primary children recite their letters, she wondered what she could do to find out more about what happened to Winslow Hopewell. When Timothy Pretlove, who was looking rather pale and sad, came to her desk to show a misshapen bird's nest he had found, she pushed it away.

"Don't put that dirty thing on my desk, Timothy," she scolded him, and then was sorry she had said it when he looked at her wonderingly.

"But look, the nest has two nests—one on top of the other." He carefully pulled aside some of the nesting material and showed her another nest below with some broken shells in it.

"So it has. I've never seen one like that. How did you discover that?"

"The nest fell down in the rain this morning. I took it into the barn and I just looked and looked until I found out why it was so funny looking. I've never seen a nest like this."

Charlotte put the nest on a windowsill where the other children could see Timothy's unusual find. He'd given her an idea. Maybe she could discover something if she looked hard enough at the place Winslow Hopewell had been found. Wasn't that what Auguste Dupin did when he wanted to figure out how the two women in Mr. Poe's story were killed? No one had searched the blueberry patch looking for clues. Maybe there was something that would tell her Mr. Platt was wrong about the tramp.

As soon as the lesson was over, she hurried back to her room to grab a shawl, and went over to the blueberry patch. As she got close to the spot where the body had been found, the ground was churned up with dozens of footprints overlapping one another. They went in all directions and covered the area except for an oblong of crushed grass where the body had been. No matter how hard she stared at the ground, Charlotte couldn't see anything that would tell her what had happened. How did Winslow Hopewell fall? Was anyone with him?

The late afternoon sun lit up the leaves of the maple trees, which were already red-tipped as autumn approached. The grove was very quiet, even the birds must have been asleep. From the road she heard the rattle of Mr. Platt's wagon coming back from his corn fields. That would be the road where the Irish tramp walked when he left the barn. If he turned from it to walk toward the grove, he must have left footprints in the mud. Were there any footprints coming in that direction?

Slowly Charlotte walked toward the road, trying to find footprints along the edges of the grassy patches. The mud was drying now, preserving the prints until the next rain. Finally she saw footprints, a man's large shoes, definitely coming from the direction of the road. But they didn't go all the way up to where the body was found. About halfway there the prints stopped behind a big chokeberry bush.

Charlotte walked carefully toward the bush. She must be careful not to make new footprints. There were plenty of prints behind the bush all mashed together, then another set heading back to the road. That would fit in with what Daniel had said earlier—that the man had seen people around a body and skedaddled. There was no way to know whether these prints were his, but maybe the sheriff could figure that out. Would he come out from the city again to take a look at the footprints?

While Charlotte searched for clues, Mrs. Ripley and some of the other women laid out Winslow Hopewell's body in the parlor. Charles Dana and John Dwight had volunteered to build a coffin. Charlotte could hear their hammers and smell the newly cut lumber as she walked back to the house. When it was finished, Reverend Hopewell's father would come and take his son's body into Boston.

There would be a grand funeral in a couple of days and no doubt Mr. Ripley and many of the other Brook Farmers would go into the city for that. Meanwhile everyone tried to carry on as though they were pretending nothing terrible had happened. Mr. Ripley said an extra prayer at grace before supper. During the meal voices were hushed; even the students talked in whispers. Abigail had put away her white dress and was wearing a black one. Her face was pale and strained.

Daniel Gallagher showed up again the next morning. He was in the kitchen when Ellen and Charlotte went down to help prepare breakfast.

"Did you find that Rory O'Connor?" Charlotte asked him.

"Find him I did. He was working at the dock, unloading molasses from a West Indies ship. I had scarcely had a chance to talk to him when along comes some farmer and the sheriff."

"That must have been Mr. Platt," Charlotte interrupted.

"Indeed it was. He was yelling 'There he is! That's the man I saw!' Rory was getting ready to run away, but he had the good sense not to do that. The sheriff asked him where he'd been in the morning and pretty soon the story came out—the same one he had told me. Mr. Platt was scowling and saying how no one could trust an Irish tramp."

"And I suppose the sheriff agreed with him," added Ellen.

"The sheriff didn't say much. He kinda grunted and said he'd take Rory down to the jail and ask him some more questions. That was the last I saw of him, but at least I know where he is."

"What will you do now?" Charlotte wanted to know. "You don't believe Rory killed Mr. Hopewell, do you? Wait until after breakfast, I have something to show you."

Just then Fanny Gray came into the kitchen. "You don't have the tables set yet," she scolded "Everyone will be down to breakfast soon. Then turning to Daniel, she added, "What are you doing here young man? We can't feed everyone who wanders in for a visit. We're very strict about the rules here."

"Sure, I had my breakfast hours ago in Boston," Daniel answered her with a smile. "I wouldn't interfere with meals, ma'am. I'll just wait outside until I have a chance to talk with Mr. Ripley."

Breakfast was another quiet meal. Charlotte finished her porridge quickly and took a piece of brown bread outside to share with Daniel Gallagher. She suspected he hadn't had any breakfast at all, no matter what he said. He must have left Boston at sunrise.

"I found Rory's footprints," she told him. "It's just like he said—he stood behind a bush and then went back to the road. If you come quickly I'll show you before I start my class."

Daniel followed her out to the spot where the body was found. She showed him the footprints coming up from the road and stopping behind the chokecherry bush. He whistled when he saw them.

"You're a clever one to notice these. We'll have to draw a picture right now so we can see whether it matches Rory's shoes." He pulled sheets of paper out of his pocket and crouched down beside the print. Using a piece of string, he measured the exact length and width of the print. His hands moved quickly but carefully getting the measurement exactly right. Then he started drawing. He frowned with concentration and his hair fell over his forehead as he worked; he pushed it back impatiently. His fingers were very long and white and his drawing was good; Charlotte wondered whether he'd had drawing lessons in Ireland.

When they got back to the house, they stopped in the parlor to pay their respects to Winslow Hopewell. Mrs. Ripley and Abigail Pretlove were sitting watch. All the women took their turns at that sharing responsibility for the body until Winslow's father took him back to Boston. Charlotte couldn't help looking at the deep gash on his forehead. Something had cut deeply all across his forehead. What would leave a mark like that?

Later that morning, as she listened to the children's lessons, the picture of Winslow Hopewell's battered face kept coming back to her. Why would anyone strike at a man like him? She knew that face would haunt her for weeks. That gash...suddenly she realized what could have caused such a deep, wide cut. It was the size of the hoes used for cultivating the crops at the Farm. Could Winslow Hopewell have been attacked with a hoe from their own barn? It was just a wild guess. But maybe it was possible. The thought made her shudder.

CHAPTER SIX

Charlotte Talks to the Sheriff

October 11, 1842

Shortly before noon, the men came from the barn carrying the new coffin. At almost the same time, a large closed carriage arrived from Boston. The Reverend Thomas Hopewell was a thin gray-haired man, his face pinched with sorrow. George Ripley helped him step down from the coach and greeted him warmly. The two men walked slowly into the parlor while Charlotte and the other women clustered around the door to offer their sympathy. The Reverend Hopewell accepted their words with a thin smile.

Before long it was over and some of the younger men carried the closed coffin from the parlor, down the front steps and slipped it into the back of the carriage. Old Mr. Hopewell's shoulders sagged as he watched them lift it, but the rigid expression on his face never changed. He shook hands with Mr. Ripley, took his place in the carriage and soon rumbled off on the road to Boston.

Classes weren't held on Wednesday afternoons, so Daniel and Charlotte decided to walk into the city and tell the sheriff about the footprints they had found. Ellen and Fred tagged along. Ellen said she had to buy pepper and nutmeg for her mother's baking, but the two of them were more interested in getting away from the bleak feeling at the farm than in buying spices.

The four of them trudged along the road while clouds gathered overhead and wind swirled dead grasses across their paths. The goldenrod had died out and the fields were brown with defeated bushes drooping toward the ground. When they got to the edge of the city, Fred and Ellen headed off for the market near the docks while Daniel and Charlotte went to the new City Hall on School Street to see the sheriff, Samuel Grover.

They found Mr. Grover sitting at a large desk poring over some papers. A skinny clerk in a black suit sat in a scratching away on a long sheet of paper copying a document. Mr. Grover stood up to greet them and Charlotte was surprised at how tall and large he was. When they told him what they wanted, he invited them to sit down and asked Daniel to explain.

"It was Miss Edgerton who thought of going to the spot and search for more clues," Daniel told him. "She found a set of prints from boots leading from the road up to the edge of the clearing where the body was found. Here's a sketch I made of the prints, so you can see whether they match Rory's boots. The prints they left show pretty clearly that the person wearing these boots didn't go close to Reverend Hopewell that morning."

Sheriff Grover sent the clerk off to bring back Rory's boots while Charlotte told him about finding the tracks. "They went from the road up toward the blueberry bushes where people were gathered, but it was muddy that morning and I could see that the prints stopped right behind the big chokecherry bush. There were a lot of prints right there, but then a line of them heading back to the road."

"You think this proves that O'Connor was just an innocent passerby?" asked the Sheriff.

"Yes, he wasn't close enough to where it happened" Daniel answered. "Besides, if he had killed Reverend Hopewell, why didn't he take the money that was in his pockets? He even had a gold pocket watch with a chain. No one could miss seeing that. Any thief would take it."

"And where would he get a hoe?" Charlotte asked. "Mr. Platt didn't say anything about seeing the tramp carrying a hoe. Where did it get to?"

By this time the clerk was back with the boots. They were pretty worn down and shabby, but the length was the same as Daniel's measurements. One of them had a hole in the sole that matched exactly the mark in the picture.

Sheriff Grover looked over the picture and the boots carefully. He even carried them to the window to get the full light.

"Yep, these look like the same boots all right," he finally agreed. "But I have to see for myself. First I have to go out there and take a look at these footprints for myself. It's curious that the money and the pocket watch weren't taken, but I have to be sure. We can't keep this man in jail much longer anyway. It costs us money to feed him. If I'm satisfied everything is the way you say it is, I'll see about setting bail. We'll still want to keep an eye on him though. You can't trust a tramp like that. They're always getting into trouble."

Daniel gritted his teeth and said nothing more to the sheriff. When he and Charlotte got outside though, he muttered. "That sheriff would love to pin a crime on Rory. He doesn't care whether the man's guilty or not. As long as he can blame some Irish tramp everyone will be satisfied."

"The only way we can be sure Rory isn't blamed," Charlotte answered, "is to find the person who is responsible. We just have to work twice as hard."

"First of all I'm going to write up this story for Mr. Cabot and see whether he'll print it in tomorrow's paper," Daniel answered. "Then we'll see what we can do for the next step."

Charlotte had agreed to meet Ellen at her aunt's house so she hurried there and found Ellen and Fred talking to Aunt Bridget and to another woman. Both women were making bonnets and scraps of bright colored fabric and velvet ribbon littered the table. As the women stretched the fabric over the bonnet frames and pulled it into place, the silk caught on their red, rough hands.

The visitor, Maura O'Malley, was an older woman with wrinkled cheeks and gray-streaked hair. She held the sewing up close to her eyes and peered at it as she worked. Ellen's cousin Maureen was threading the needle for her, but no matter how weak her eyes were her stitches were quick and strong. She listened without saying anything while Fred talked about the events at Brook Farm.

"Poor Mr. Hopewell," exclaimed Mrs. O'Malley when he had finished. "I remember when he was a young man he used to visit at the house where I worked. Handsome, he was, and so well-spoken. Old Miss Coffin and her niece loved having him come for tea, and he always appreciated my soda bread."

"Miss Coffin was the Quaker woman you worked for, wasn't she?" asked Aunt Bridget. "It's a pity she died. You don't find many employers as generous as she was."

"She was good to me, 'tis true. But I did a few good turns for her too. There's many a time a servant is worth more than gold to her mistress."

"Servants don't often get paid for it though," said Fred. "Don't seamstresses hate having to spend every minute sewing bonnets and dresses for ladies who pay so little? We have to change things in this world so everyone shares instead of rich people having everything."

"You're talking like a true Brook Farmer now, Fred" Ellen added. "I don't know that anything we do at the Farm is going to help the seamstresses in Boston."

"Brook Farm," mused Mrs. O'Malley. "They have some wild ideas, don't they? And Abigail Coffin—Pretlove she is now—lives out there, doesn't she? I hope she finds herself a good husband. She's had troubles enough and a good husband is the best cure for that."

Fred was all set to start on a long rant about changing the world, but the others hurried him off so they could get back to the Farm before dark. There were so many questions to answer about Winston Hopewell's death. There was no time to linger in Boston.

The long trek back to the Farm was tiring and the three of them barely made it in time for supper. Fanny Gray was already putting the plates and tableware out and Charlotte was sure she'd be cross that they hadn't been there to help. Oddly enough, she didn't say anything as they came in and started carrying bowls of food into the dining room. Fanny looked up briefly, but her face was blotchy as though she had been crying and her eyes looked at them blankly. Charlotte wondered briefly if she had been particularly fond of Reverend Hopewell and was very sad about his end. But surely the handsome Winslow Hopewell would not have spent much time thinking about poor Fanny with her graying hair and pinched face.

The dining room was quiet again that evening. Even the youngest students could feel that something terrible had happened. Their eyes were fastened on the adults as though they were waiting for someone to explain things to them. Timothy Pretlove wiggled uncomfortably on his chair and looked down at his plate, scarcely touching his food. Every once in a while he would glance at his mother, but Abigail was silent and absorbed in her own thoughts.

When the meal was over, Mr. Ripley stood up to make an announcement. "We in the Community have had a great shock and sorrow. We have lost a good friend in the most horrifying way. Some outsider has found his way into our happy group and brought evil to us, but the sheriff is trying to discover the perpetrator. We must continue our work and go about our business, secure in the faith that we will root out this evil and survive.

"One of the Community's friends is coming to visit us on Friday. Margaret Fuller was a member of the group whose meetings led to the establishment of Brook Farm. Her visit was arranged long before the tragedy occurred. It will do us all good to meet again with one of the most respected women in our state. Let us all try to put aside our sorrow for the time being and welcome her."

Margaret Fuller! Charlotte and Ellen were excited by the thought of seeing her. She was said to be one of the brightest women in America. For years she had conducted meetings of women in Boston; conversations she called them, where women including Mrs. Ripley and Lydia Maria Child had met together and talked about the kind of ideas that men studied at Harvard.

While the girls helped clear the tables and take the dishes to the kitchen, Charlotte noticed that even Fanny Gray looked more cheerful. As the two of them washed and dried the dishes together, Fanny said, "I went to Margaret Fuller's conversations in Boston one year. It was because of her that I decided to follow Sophia and George Ripley and move to Brook Farm."

"Does Margaret Fuller approve of our radical ideas?" asked Charlotte. "Why doesn't she join the Community?"

"That's the question I keep asking myself," Fanny answered frowning again as she thought about it. "Her support would help us greatly. She influences so many people. Why does she avoid joining us in our great enterprise?"

CHAPTER SEVEN

Abigail Thinks About Secrets

October 12, 1842

As the carriage carrying Winslow's body rolled down the road, Abigail shivered. Her stomach felt hollow. For eight years she had not seen him; he had disappeared from her life, but in the few weeks since his arrival he had again become a part of it. Just two months ago she had felt strong on her own, but all the secrets she had buried for years swarmed out when Winslow appeared again. Now they hummed around her head like midges at the lake as she paced in her small room feeling trapped.

Timothy burst into the room and demanded, "Will you walk down to the road with me so I can collect some milkweed stems? Miss Gray is going to show us how to make rope out of them."

Fresh air was just what she needed. She picked up a shawl, tied on a bonnet, and walked with Timothy and his friend John Parsons toward the road below the Hive. A mist lay over the distant hills and the sun was sinking lower, but it was still warm on her shoulders as they crunched through the dry weeds. The boys soon found plenty of milkweed stalks and began to break off the stalks and stack them in a large pile.

Mr. Platt, the farmer, was plodding along the road toward them. He had a bunch of papers in his hand and must have been coming from the post office. His shoulders were drooping, but he straightened up and smiled when he saw them.

"G'Day, Miz Pretlove," he said, touching his straw hat briefly. "What are you folks doing out this afternoon?"

"We're collecting milkweed," said Timothy excitedly. "Miss Gray is going to help us make cord to tie up packages and things."

"Looks like you'll get plenty of milkweeds here," said the farmer. "That's the only thing that's growing good this year. The corn harvest is short and Miz Platt's vegetables are drying up before they ripen. It's going to be another bad year."

"The harvest has been poor on our farm too," Abigail said. And then, trying to cheer him up, added "Did you get any good news in the mail?"

"Good news?" he snorted. "It's been a long time since I've heard any of that. My brother went out to Pennsylvania a couple of years back. Heard there was cheap land and lots of jobs building that big canal system from Philadelphia to the Ohio River at Pittsburgh. I told him it would come to this."

"Come to what, Mr. Platt?"

"Re-pu-di-a-tion, that's what it's come to. Pennsylvania borrowed so much money it couldn't pay the bonds and now the banks have collapsed. That canal won't never get built, nor the railroads neither. There's no work. No one will buy back the land. And no one will invest. Do you know what they're singing in England these days?" He read from a grimy newspaper he was carrying.

"Yankee Doodle borrows cash,

Yankee Doodle spends it,

And then he snaps his fingers at

The jolly flat who lends it.

Ask him when he means to pay,

He shews no hesitation,

But says he'll take the shortest way,

And that's repudiation!

Mr. Platt sighed as he folded up the paper. "What's a man to do? My brother can hardly feed his family."

"Maybe your brother can come back to Massachusetts. Times are bad here, but quite a few people have joined Community and are hoping to make a new start that way."

Mr. Platt snorted again. "There are too many radicals in your Community with their queer ideas. How are they ever going to make a success of a farm? Most of them don't know one end of a cow from the other."

His voice was so gruff and bleak that Abigail didn't have the heart to say anything. Maybe he was right. A few years ago everyone had been so hopeful, but the great changes they had wanted weren't coming. She thought again of Winslow and how he had looked when she first met him. Tears stung her eyes and she turned quickly to the boys.

"Come on Timothy, come on John, we have to get back now." Dark gray storm clouds were rolling in and the sun was sinking fast. A chilly wind tugged at her shawl. They said good-by to Mr. Platt and turned toward the Hive.

The boys wanted to show their treasures to Fanny Gray, so they walked up to the schoolroom. She was sitting at the teacher's desk reading a newspaper by the light of a small lamp, but she looked up as they walked in.

"You boys have done well collecting all these," she said cheerfully enough. "Why don't you lay them carefully on the floor under that window so they can dry out some more overnight."

Fanny had never been a pretty woman, but tonight she looked worse than ever. The lamplight revealed more wrinkles in her face than Abigail had ever noticed before. Frown lines furrowed her forehead and deep lines cut into her cheeks and pulled her mouth down. She pushed her hair back from her forehead and tried to smile.

"Timothy is such a curious boy and always eager to learn. He's a good example to the other children in the class," she said. She paused and then added, "Not like the politicians we've been sending to Congress I must say."

"What have they been up to?" Abigail asked. "Is that a recent paper you have?"

"My sister sends it to me every month. Her husband is a Congressman from Salem. Do you know what has been going on in Washington? President Tyler and Congress can't seem to agree on anything. When the president vetoed the bank bill last month his entire Cabinet resigned and walked out on him. All except Daniel Webster that is."

"How can the government go on?" Abigail was truly alarmed.

"I don't know," Fanny was almost wailing now and her voice trembled. "We must save ourselves. The whole country seems to be falling apart with banks failing and states unable to pay their bills. My uncle put all of his savings into Pennsylvania bonds and now they are worthless. Will Massachusetts be next? Those of us who have come together in our Community must work to make it strong so we can maintain ourselves without depending on banks or governments." She sounded so desperate that even Timothy and John looked at her.

Fortunately the supper bell started chiming and they had to hurry downstairs. It was good to get away from the gloomy light of the schoolroom.

The lamplight in the dining room flickered on the long tables and reflected off the white napkin laid beside each plate. Abigail sat next to Charlotte who would be a more cheerful companion than Fanny Gray. Charlotte told Abigail about her trip to Boston to see the sheriff.

"I think we convinced Sheriff Grover that Rory O'Connor is not a murderer. The sheriff is still suspicious of him though. It sounds as though he doesn't trust anyone who is Irish. He says he's going to keep an eye on Mr. O'Connor. There will always be suspicions until the real culprit is found."

"Oh, and Abigail," she added, "I met someone you know. Someone who worked for your aunt and knew you when you lived in Boston. What was her name? Maura O'Malley. She seemed a friendly woman and asked to be remembered to you."

"Maura O'Malley?" Abigail echoed. Charlotte was startled to see her cheeks flush as she looked down at her plate

CHAPTER EIGHT

Daniel Has an Idea

October 14, 1842

Daniel was proud of the story he wrote about the mysterious death at the Brook Farm community. Mr. Cabot ran it on the front page of Thursday's paper and had more copies printed than usual. Sales were brisk. As he walked to the newspaper office Daniel saw a newsboy on almost every corner peddling the papers and they were going fast.

One of the young Harvard boys caught up with him as they got to the office. His wire-rimmed eyeglasses glittered as he sneered, "I guess you're used to getting up at dawn and running around the docks chasing stories. I only write about gentlemen."

Mr. Cabot came into the office about 10 o'clock. With him was a stout man wearing a top hat and with the largest, heaviest looking gold watch chain Daniel had ever seen across his vest. As he walked past the clerks he pulled his watch out and Daniel caught a glimpse of the heavy gold case with a flashing diamond set in the center. Was it cotton or molasses that had earned all that wealth? The man stayed in the office a long time, but when he came out at last Daniel grabbed the chance to say a word to Mr. Cabot.

"Now that Rory O'Connor is not being charged with the murder of the Reverend Hopewell, I'd like to look into the story further and write it up for the paper. If you could give me a letter saying I was working for the *Transcript* that might encourage people to talk to me."

"Are you thinking of going out to talk to people in that Community, young man? That won't get you anyplace. I'm sure George Ripley and his friends have nothing to do with a crime like this. You'd better look for the disreputable elements in the city. Talk to those Irish laborers down by the docks or maybe the freedmen at the African Baptist Church. They would be more likely to have heard about troublemakers coming into the area." Mr. Cabot's thin lips twisted as he spat out the word "troublemakers".

"I'll talk to everyone I can, sir, but I'd like to look around the Farm first and see whether anyone saw strangers lurking about."

In the end Mr. Cabot had his clerk write a short letter which he signed it with a bold flourish. As he handed it to Daniel, he said, "I am trusting you not to bring disgrace on the *Transcript*, so you had better watch your behavior."

Daniel forced himself to smile and he kept his thoughts to himself as he thanked Mr. Cabot and took the letter. He decided to walk over to the jail to see whether Rory was still being held. He turned into an alley to take a shortcut to City Hall, but stopped abruptly when he saw a scuffle up ahead.

"Leave me be!" shouted a voice. Daniel knew he should turn back, but instead he hurried ahead. "We don't need troublemakers like you here," yelled another voice. "Go back where you came from!"

Daniel recognized Rory facing off against three rough-looking workmen. He couldn't turn his back on him. "Leave him alone." His voice startled the fighters.

The three attackers turned and saw they were caught between him and Rory. They pushed past Rory toward the end of the alley and disappeared. Daniel glared after them, but was just as glad he didn't have to get into a fight. Not with his good clothes on.

"What was going on?" he asked.

Rory wiped a bit of blood from a cut on his face and answered, "My cousin came to say a good word for me and the sheriff let me out of jail on her say-so. These men would rather see me hang for something I didn't do. Sure they're afraid the Irish are taking over their precious city."

The story was all too familiar to Daniel. Another reason he was determined to work out who was really responsible for the young minister's death. Someone must be held accountable for a terrible crime like that. Otherwise there would always be suspicions about Rory, about all the Irish. Besides, if he could figure what had happened, what a feather in his cap that would be! No one would sneer at him then.

The walk out to the Farm was a long one, but the weather was bright and sunny and there was a lot to think about on the way. The stands of maple along the road were blazing with color, red and gold leaves tossing in the air. That was one thing Massachusetts had over Galway, the color of its autumn. Daniel remembered looking out the cottage door at home at the rocky fields leading to the cliffs. As soon as the green of summer was gone, everything looked gray—the barren fields, the rocky cliffs and the gray-green water battering the shore. Here there was a month of fiery leaves to brighten the landscape until winter came and the snow.

As he tramped along the road Daniel hummed to himself the song his father used to sing so often:

A nation once again, a nation once again

And Ireland long a province be a nation once again

Ireland might become a nation, but Daniel wasn't waiting around for it to happen. His father had talked a lot about the glory days of 1798 when he had fought against the British, but Ireland had lost. American won its fight and formed its own country. Daniel would take his chances with the new world and let poor old Ireland sink or swim on its own. His father had grown withered and bitter with the years. He died waiting for justice, but Daniel was determined to prosper. His dreams were bright. He'd bring his mother and sisters over to a new country. How surprised they'd be when they saw him in a suit and wearing a cravat—a respected newspaper man.

Ahead on the road he could see the farmer who had been in the barnyard at the Farm last time he was there. When he caught up with him, Daniel wished him a good day and walked along next to him. The farmer nodded but didn't say a word of greeting.

"You must be a great help to the people in the Brook Farm Community," Daniel said, trying to get him talking. He didn't take the bait, but just grunted.

"They could hardly get along without you, I'd think, because none of them are farmers, even though some of them are very well-known people."

"Not farmers indeed!" Mr. Platt finally exploded. "Do you know that no one on the place will slaughter a pig for themselves, though they're happy enough to eat the pork? They don't even like to wring the neck of a chicken. Humpf! My ten-year-old boy can do that much!"

"They have lots of strange ideas. No doubt about that."

"Lots of crazy ideas, I call them" Mr. Platt was getting red in the face now and he shook the hoe he was carrying as though he'd like to hit someone with it. "What right have they to come in and tell us how to live? Everyone should milk their cows in the morning and then go off and write a book for the rest of the day they say. That's nonsense! I milk my cows and then tend to my oats and corn. With grain prices the way they are these days there's no time for writing books."

He was scowling now and not giving Daniel a chance to get a word in edgewise. "And then they're saying we should let those African freedmen come in and work our land. And the slovenly Irish! They'll take the land away from honest Americans. They're a menace to the state."

"Why do you help the Brook Farmers then?"

"They're neighbors. Can't let 'em starve. Besides, they pay me for the use of my wagon and tools. Or they used to. Now they're short of money they say and old George Ripley keeps putting off the paying." Once again he scowled. "Lots of people come out here to see them, but I don't think there's many putting any money into the Farm."

When Daniel got to the farm, the noon dinner was just over. The washing-up group was in the kitchen making quick work of the dishes. He asked about Mr. Ripley and was told he was closeted in his office talking with Charles Dana and some of the other men. When he caught a glimpse of Charlotte in the dining room, he walked over to talk with her. She was standing at a table fussing with some dried leaves she was arranging in a vase. Two other women were with her; one he recognized as the cross-looking woman who had shooed him out of the kitchen the other morning and the other one was a lovely young woman he'd never seen before. She was dressed in black and had glossy black hair gathered in a bunch at the back of her neck. When she looked at him, her eyes were bright blue and her cheeks so pale and smooth she reminded him of the picture of the Madonna h*e'd seen in church. Charlotte introduced her as Abigail Pretlove.*

"Did you know that Margaret Fuller was coming to visit us today?" Charlotte asked, pushing her hair back from her forehead. "She is one of the most famous women in Massachusetts,"

"We all admire Margaret Fuller," added Mrs. Pretlove. Her voice was soft but firm. "She's so clever she inspires us all. And she thinks women ought to speak up for themselves."

Charlotte chimed in. "You can hear her speak this afternoon. And then you can write a story about her for your newspaper, that is, if people in Boston are interested in what we are doing out here."

"They are more interested in how the Reverend Hopewell died." Daniel decided not to mention the men who had roughed up Rory. "Everyone in Boston is wondering who to blame. They certainly swooped up the papers yesterday with my story in it." Daniel tried not to sound boastful saying that.

"We all care deeply about Mr. Hopewell's death," Abigail spoke again. "But we are trying to carry on as he would have wished. He was a friend of Margaret Fuller's too. She published one of his essays in her new magazine, *The Dial.* He would have wanted us to welcome her to the Community."

"Come into the parlor, Mr. Gallagher. She will be speaking in a few minutes," Charlotte urged. She led the way into the parlor. About a dozen men and women sat in chairs around the room talking quietly to one another, while some of the older students sprawled on the floor. Mr. and Mrs. Ripley came into the room through the large, double doors. Between them walked a small woman holding a stick with eyeglasses on it and peering around the room. Miss Fuller was not beautiful, but she walked as though she were. Her glance swept the room, friendly and yet impersonal. As she took her chair at the front, she arranged her flowing dark red skirt around her and draped her black silk shawl gracefully across her shoulders. No one could look at anyone but her.

After taking her place at a table in the front of the room, Margaret Fuller leaned forward and began to speak.

"You have all suffered a dreadful loss," she said. "The unexpected death here at Brook Farm has shaken us all. In a community dedicated to building a better world, no one would expect such a terrible thing to happen. What could have brought such evil into our world?"

"It's all the outsiders we're letting into the neighborhood," interrupted the farmer. "It was one of those Irish tramps that killed the reverend. I don't care what the sheriff says. They're lazy, shiftless people who would rather lie than tell the honest truth."

Margaret Fuller frowned at the interruption, but she plunged ahead. "What do you expect of a people who have been oppressed for centuries? These are the faults of an oppressed race, which must require the aid of better circumstances through two or three generations to eradicate. Can you not appreciate their virtues? They have strong family ties, they are generous, and have indefatigable good-

humor and ready wit. They are fundamentally one of the best na-
tions of the world."

She paused and looked around at the audience, but no one said a
word. Then she continued:

"If only the Irish were welcomed here, not to work merely, but
to find intelligent sympathy as they struggle patiently and ardently
for the education of their children! No sympathy could be better
deserved, no efforts better timed. Will you not believe it, merely
because that bog-bred youth you placed in the mud-hole tells you
lies, and drinks to cheer himself in those endless diggings? You are
short-sighted; you do not look to the future; you will not turn your
head to see what may have been the influences of the past. You have
not examined your own breast to see whether the monitor there has
not commanded you to do your part to counteract these influences;
and yet the Irishman appeals to you, eye to eye."

Mr. Platt didn't have any answer for that flow of eloquence. Daniel smiled to think how this little woman had silenced him, but he
knew the farmer wasn't convinced. He still thought Rory O'Connor
or someone like him had killed the Reverend.

For a while the ladies in the parlor listened to Miss Fuller and
asked a few questions about Irish servants and the best way to edu-
cate them and help them learn to read and write and to act like
Americans. Daniel became restless waiting for a chance to talk with
Mr. Ripley, but there was no opening.

When Mr. Ripley declared the meeting over, he walked out of
the room with his wife and Margaret Fuller and Daniel had no
chance to talk to him. Gradually the group broke up into small
clumps of women talking with one another. Charlotte and Abigail
walked toward Daniel.

"Are you going to write the story up for the newspaper?" asked Charlotte.

"Not too many people in Boston want to read about how to be good to your servants," he answered. "Not much excitement in that."

"Mr. Platt's interruption disturbed me," Abigail Pretlove added. "That man is full of anger."

"What's he worried about? No one is trying to take away his farm."

"But he's afraid nonetheless," insisted Abigail. "I met him on the road yesterday and he was talking about how the country is falling apart. His brother has lost a lot of money because Pennsylvania repudiated their bond debt. Maybe Mr. Platt thinks it will happen to him."

"He'd fight back if anybody tried to take anything away from him." Daniel responded, thinking about how fierce he had looked on the road shaking his hoe and talking about the Brook Farmers. "I'd hate to meet him on a dark road some night."

Thinking about darkness made Daniel realize he wouldn't have a chance to talk to Mr. Ripley today. He had a good two-hour walk ahead of him and if he didn't watch out, his boarding house would be locked for the night. There was a lot to think about on the way to Boston.

CHAPTER NINE

Abigail Tells a Story

October 16, 1842

Sundays at Brook Farm were busy and noisy. Sometimes a visiting preacher gave a sermon to a small group in the parlor; other days John Dwight would gather some of the students together to sing hymns. Always there was talking and music and singing. It was all very pleasant, but at times Abigail missed the quiet of the Sunday mornings when she was a child in Philadelphia.

She used to walk with mother and father to the Quaker Meeting House for First Day worship. How proud she was when her father decided she was old enough to sit and be quiet with the grown-ups for the service. The silence might be broken when one of the adults stood up and said something odd, "I saw a red-winged blackbird spring from her nest by Foxglove creek this morning and my heart was filled with the wonder of God's grace." Abigail would look at the sun streaming into the small worship room and wonder whether that was God's grace, or whether she would ever really know if it was. The silence was mysterious, but comforting and when the service was over she felt strangely contented.

On the Sunday after Winslow died Abigail decided to walk to Boston with Timothy. The news about Maura O'Malley had unsettled her. It was years since she had seen Mrs. O'Malley. What a godsend she had been when Timothy was born. What would have happened if Aunt Phoebe hadn't been able to call on Maura O'Malley at that terrible time? As Abigail walked along the quiet Sunday road she remembered driving out into the country with Maura and her nephew—Patrick, his name was. It was June and she was hot and sick and scared as the wagon jolted over the rutted road. Maura put her arm around her and rocked her as though she was a baby while her nephew kept singing to the horse.

Patrick and his wife Clare were cheerful and the three little children running around kept Abigail occupied. Maura got her through the birth. She didn't remember much about that except the moment when she first held Timothy and realized he was going to be with her for the rest of her life. She watched him now, running a stick through the grass at the side of the road, looking serious as he searched for jump-toads and bugs. Tears stung her eyes—he looked just the way Winslow had looked when he talked about all those books he read. She didn't want to think about that. She had to keep going.

When they reached Boston, she searched for the house where Maura used to live. What if she had moved? The house was so weather-beaten it was impossible to tell what color it had been originally and the front steps listed to one side like a derelict rowboat on the river. But the knocker was brightly polished and made a satisfying klunk when Abigail used it.

Soon the door opened and there was Maura, a little plumper and a little grayer than she had been eight years ago, but her smile was as friendly as ever. "Abigail, child, it's a treat to see you. Sure you're as beautiful as you always were and don't look a day older than when all the young men were buzzing around you in your aunt's parlor. And this can't be Timothy, can it? Such a handsome boy!" She hugged Abigail close and reached down to hug Timothy, although he squirmed away shyly.

She urged them into the house and led them down a dark hallway to the kitchen. "Sit down at the table and I'll make you some tea. I'm just back from mass and some tea and cakes will taste very good."

In the kitchen a boy about Timothy's age was playing at marbles on the floor. "This is young Pat, one of my nephew's boys." And turning to him she added "Pat, why don't you and Timothy go out into the back alley and play with those marbles so you're not underfoot?"

The boys darted out quick as a flash. Abigail sank into a chair gratefully, suddenly feeling how tired she was from the long walk. She could tell Maura was looking at her black dress and wondering about it.

"Still wearing black, are you?" Maura asked. "You were a widow when Timothy was born. That's a long time for a young woman to be in mourning."

Her comforting voice melted something in Abigail and she felt tears threatening again. She wanted to tell her everything that had happened, to talk to her the way she used to talk to her aunt. Her voice quavered as she started, "I wasn't really a widow then. That was a story Aunt Phoebe and I made up for the world to know."

"Well, don't worry about it. Many's the girl has to make up a story and there's none should ask too many questions. The great thing is that you have Timothy now and he's a fine boy you can be proud of." She poured out a cup of tea and put it on the table. "I never really thought you were a widow—and you so young. It's hard sometimes to wait for a wedding ring with a girl so beautiful that all the men are hanging around her."

That really started Abigail's tears going. She was glad Timothy couldn't see her as she gulped them down. "I was married. I really was. But Winslow changed. He didn't believe in it at all. How could he say a marriage wasn't a real marriage?"

Maura handed her a slice of bread slathered with jam. "A marriage is a marriage I would have thought. What in heaven's name was wrong with it?"

"You know we're Quakers, my family. We don't have marriages in churches. If a man and woman declare before God that they are man and wife, then they are married. Of course, you're supposed to tell your Meeting about your plans and have the elders approve. We didn't do that. Winslow's father would have disowned him for marrying a Quaker. So we walked over to the river very early one morning when the sun was coming up. Winslow picked some violets and gave them to me. I remember a robin was bursting with song in the tree over our head. We held each other by the hand and affirmed that we were man and wife. That was marriage enough for us."

"And did you not tell your aunt?" asked Maura as she poured more tea.

"No, Winslow wanted it to be our secret and we were so happy for a while. Then his father started talking to him about taking a pulpit and being a preacher like all the men in the family. How could a Boston minister have a Quaker for a wife? I knew he was thinking that." She had to stop and blow her nose.

"But with a baby coming. He didn't leave you, did he?" Maura leaned over the table.

"We didn't know about the baby. I told him to go do what his father told him if that's what he wanted. I was so angry I don't know what I said, but I know I said some horrible things about him being a little boy always doing what his father told him." The words hurt her throat as she said them. "And he went. He just went away!" She had to stop talking because the tears were coming so fast. And that was just the time Timothy and his friend came in from the alley.

Timothy looked scared when he saw his mother crying. He came over and stood next to her and wrapped his arm around her neck. "It's all right, it's all right," she reassured him. "Mother's just telling a sad story. Don't pay any attention. See, I'm smiling now." She tried to force her face to smile. Maura bustled around getting tea for the boys and spreading a piece of bread and jam for each of them. Soon young Pat took Timothy off in one corner to show him some special yellow marbles.

Abigail felt better despite the storm of tears. She had held the story inside herself ever since her aunt died. She had pretended to be a widow for so long that she almost believed it herself and her fantasy husband, poor George Pretlove who had died at sea, seemed almost real. During the years when she and her aunt lived in Groton no one had questioned her story.

Over the years she sometimes heard news about Winslow and his preaching. He never knew about Timothy until he visited Brook Farm. After that Abigail finally told him the truth. He was shattered by the news—angry at first and then terribly sad that he had missed years with his son. They were just beginning to talk about making changes. Then came that terrible morning.

When Abigail and Timothy left, Maura hugged them and made them promise to come back and visit again soon. Pat even gave Timothy a small blue and white marble to keep for his own. And when they were leaving, Maura went off and came back with a small piece of cloth wrapped around something that she pressed into Abigail's hand. "Sure God always has his eye on you, Abigail. Don't you ever worry about that. Timothy is a gift from Him and you will be happy again. I know you will."

When she unwrapped the cloth Abigail found a rosary made of worn beads with pieces of yarn tied to mark the decades. She only recognized what it was because Maura had given it to her to hold onto during the birth. She said it would calm her. And it had. She had survived that; maybe she would get through these difficult days too.

Timothy held her hand as they walked along the quiet road back to the Farm. He seemed to know she was feeling sad and lonesome. Soon Abigail began reciting to him some of the poetry her father used to read to her years before. The autumn fields were brown and dreary, but she remembered some lines from Keats:

Where are the songs of Spring? Ay, where are they?
Think not of them, thou hast thy music too,--
While barred clouds bloom the soft-dying day,
And touch the stubble-plains with rosy hue;
[Something something she could not remember and then]
And gathering swallows twitter in the skies.

There were no swallows in these skies, but other birds were twittering in the trees, making soft, comforting sounds. Maybe things would be better. She was still young and she had Timothy. This year was dying, but another year would come—many other years. Winslow was silent and gone. They would never talk again, but she and Timothy were alive.

.

CHAPTER TEN

Charlotte Hears a Secret

October. 17, 1842

On Monday, the rain came down in a slow, drizzle of water that soaked Charlotte's shoes as she walked across the lawn to the Hive. The few leaves remaining on the trees hung limply, waiting to be swirled away to their deaths, and the sharp wind was a reminder that winter was well on its way. Margaret Fuller had left the Farm on Sunday afternoon, busy until the last minute talking with Mr. and Mrs. Ripley. Charlotte, like many others, wished she could have stayed longer. It would be wonderful to know as much as she did and be so respected as well as loved.

The children in the primary class were restless as they always were on rainy days. Johnny Parsons twisted around in his seat to make a face at little Mary Miller, who stuck her tongue out in retaliation. It was tiresome having to remind them to act like ladies and gentlemen, as if they could at that age. If the sun had been shining Charlotte would have taken them all out to look for spider webs and shake the cobwebs out of their brains after reading the fable "The Spider and the Silkworm". Since they had to stay indoors, she decided they could look for spider webs in the attic. She pretended they were starting on an exploring trip and led them up the wooden stairs to the large, dusty room under the eaves. Two small windows, one at each end of the room, gave a dim gray light through dusty windows. Along the sides of the room, under the slanting eaves, large trunks and bulky packages, some of them draped in sheeting, were stored.

The children began to search in all the corners, the boys giggling and teasing the girls about being frightened of spiders, but they had scarcely started when they heard someone climbing the stairs. Charlotte was relieved to see it was Abigail; she was unlikely to complain about the children's noise. She smiled at all of them. Timothy, of course, ran over to grab his mother's hand and show her the web he had found.

Abigail and Charlotte spread out one of the covering sheets and sat on the window ledge while they let the children scamper around the storeroom. Some of them were forgetting about the spider webs, but it was good for them to stretch their legs. Abigail looked less sad than she had seemed for the past week, ever since Reverend Hopewell died. She certainly took that death very hard and Charlotte wondered how she had felt about him.

She broached the subject carefully. "Did you go to Winslow Hopewell's funeral on Saturday?"

"No, I didn't," Abigail answered rather sharply. "I had no need of a funeral to make me remember him."

"Did you know him in Boston? I remember when he first arrived you said that you and he had met before."

"Yes, he used to visit my aunt's house when I lived with her. He was a charming young man, just finishing Harvard College. His father was a famous preacher, you know, and he wanted Winslow to follow in his footsteps. Winslow told me he wanted to be a poet, but in the end he followed his father's wishes." Her voice was tinged with bitterness.

"You must have known him well."

"Oh yes, I knew him very well." She turned her head to the side and Charlotte thought for a moment she was going to cry, but instead she answered in a low voice, "He said he wanted to marry me."

"But you refused him. You married Mr. Pretlove instead."

"Oh, Mr. Pretlove. The famous George Pretlove," now Abigail's voice was anguished. She took a handkerchief out of her pocket and touched it to her eyes, then held it in her hand twisting it round and round into a sausage of white linen. Charlotte wondered why she was so upset, but she said nothing.

"There was no George Pretlove. It was Winslow I was married to," suddenly burst from Abigail's mouth as though she couldn't hold it in any longer.

Charlotte could only stare at her. What did she mean there was no George Pretlove? Timothy Pretlove was her son. How could she be married to Winslow? He was a minister. Everyone would know if he had a wife.

"You mustn't tell anyone, Charlotte. I didn't mean to tell you. You can't understand and neither can anyone else. Promise me you won't tell!" She leaned toward Charlotte. Her eyes were wide with fear and her grip was like a vise.

"I won't tell," Charlotte promised. It was hard to believe the change that had come over Abigail. She was always so beautiful, so poised and quiet as though she had never any care on her mind. Charlotte had envied the easy life she led. Now she was pleading with her to keep a secret. They sat there a minute or two more just looking at each other, but then the children got tired of chasing spider webs and Charlotte had to take them back to the classroom. Abigail disappeared into her room.

Soon it was time to dismiss the children from class. It had been a long day for the smaller ones. To Charlotte's surprise Daniel was standing in the hall downstairs. For a minute he seemed like a stranger. He looked just the same as before—thin and pale with those bright blue eyes. His smile hadn't changed and that was reassuring.

"You're back again. You'll wear out the road walking back and forth so much. Have you discovered anything new about what happened to Winslow Hopewell?"

"I didn't want to bother Mr. Ripley on a Sunday, especially because you people had a famous visitor here. But I wanted to get his permission to ask questions here." Daniel was standing very straight and he had a little smile on his lips as though he was quite satisfied with himself.

"You look happy, so you must have been given the permission. And have you started asking questions yet?"

"I talked with Mr. Ripley, of course, and asked him what he knew about Winslow Hopewell and whether anyone could have been very angry with him. But I didn't learn much. Mr. Ripley knows Winslow's father. Has known him all his life. Everyone in Boston knows everyone else it seems, except for those of us who know no one. Anyway Mr. Ripley has known the Reverend Thomas Hopewell for many years. According to Mr. Ripley, he is one of the most respected men in the city and no one has a word to say against him. Winslow has been a little more controversial because there are some people who believe he is too liberal in his teaching about the

New Testament. And he has half the women in Boston pestering their husbands about the sufferings of the slaves in the South. None of that sounds as though it would get him killed, does it?"

Charlotte wondered whether one of those henpecked husbands might have killed Winslow just to stop the pestering, but that thought slid out of her mind as soon as it came in. It was too horrible to joke about when she could still see Winslow's white face in her mind.

"No, that doesn't get us very far. Is the whole family perfect? What about Mr. Hopewell's mother and brothers and sisters?"

"His mother died when he was ten years old and there were no other children. Thomas Hopewell never remarried and his son never married, so there have been no women in the family for many years."

"Oh, yes there were," Charlotte started to say and then caught herself. She couldn't betray Abigail even though she didn't know what the story about being married to Winslow meant. How could they be married if no one knew about it? She hurried to try to correct the mistake. "I mean, there were women who admired Winslow. Remember how Fanny said once that he had women swooning over his sermons? Maybe some of them were jealous."

"Silly women flutter over good looking ministers all the time," said Daniel loftily, "but they don't kill them. And none of those Boston women would have been out here at the Farm. Winslow Hopewell was a well-known and respected minister. Mr. Ripley knew him all his life from when he was a child. It's unlikely he had any guilty secrets in his life."

"Everyone has secrets. No one knows about them because they are secret. But sometimes secrets come back to haunt people."

"What do you mean? Do you think that Winslow belonged to some secret group the way my father did in Ireland? Was he a radical abolitionist? You don't think that Winslow stole church funds, do you? His family had plenty of money. What kind of secret do you think he might have had?"

"I certainly don't think he was a revolutionary or a thief," Charlotte said scornfully. "If he had a secret it was more likely to be about someone he loved or...oh, I don't know. Don't ask me." She turned away, but Daniel reached out and caught her arm.

"You know something you aren't telling me. What is it? Didn't we agree we'd try to solve this mystery together? How can we do that if you don't share what you know?"

"I can't. I just can't! And I won't say another word." She turned and ran upstairs. Her heart was pounding and if she stayed down there any longer she was afraid she would give away Abigail's secret. Daniel just stood at the bottom of the stairs watching her. He was scowling with disappointment and confusion. Charlotte didn't want to quarrel with him, but what could she do?

Thinking about darkness made Daniel realize he wouldn't have a chance to talk to Mr. Ripley today. He had a good two-hour walk ahead of him and if he didn't watch out, his boarding house would be locked for the night. There was a lot to think about on the way to Boston.

CHAPTER ELEVEN

Daniel Learns Something New

October 17-19, 1842

The rain had let up when Daniel left the Farm, but it was a damp, clammy evening with a wind that blew right through his jacket. His small lantern didn't give much light and a couple of times he nearly stumbled into a ditch. But it wasn't the deepening darkness and the ditches that made him start cussing; it was thinking about Charlotte Edgerton and why she had hinted at secrets she didn't want to tell. Had she changed her mind about working together? Were women really as changeable as that? He remembered a poem he'd read somewhere;

Must not a woman be

A feather on the sea,

Sway'd to and fro by every wind and tide?

Were women really like that? Daniel had his doubts. His mother was certainly no feather on the sea and he would never have thought of Charlotte that way either. But why had she suddenly refused to talk? What had come over her? One minute she was smiling and her dark eyes were sparkling, then suddenly they were opaque and he couldn't tell what she was thinking.

The next morning Daniel went to the newspaper office to see whether Mr. Cabot had any stories he could cover. When he admitted he hadn't uncovered any news at Brook Farm, he got a cold reception. Grudgingly Mr. Cabot sent him to the court house to find something worth writing about.

Puddles from yesterday's rain lingered in the gutters and Daniel walked carefully to avoid a dead dog stinking up the street. He couldn't afford to step into anything that would ruin his only pair of shoes. It was trouble enough keeping them shined so they didn't disgrace him or the newspaper. As he approached the gray granite courthouse Daniel could see a handful of men standing around the steps waving cigars in the air as they talked.

"Tradesmen to the back door," one of them called out as Daniel started toward the steps.

"I'm with the Boston *Transcript*", he answered, mimicking the nasal Boston accent. These Boston voices grated on him.

No one stopped him as he walked through the big wooden doors and down the echoing hallway. He was surprised there were so few clerks or lawyers in sight. One young clerk in a bright blue jacket tacking up a broadsheet outside the sheriff's office was the only person he saw, so he wandered over to read the sheet.

"Jailbreak!" was the headline in thick black letters. "Roger Platt wanted by the Sheriff of Suffolk County. This convicted debtor escaped from his cell and is thought to be in the vicinity of West Roxbury. All citizens are required to report his whereabouts if they see him."

Roger Platt—that name sounded familiar. Wasn't the farmer out by the Community named Platt? "Does this man live around here?" he asked the boy.

"I heard he was connected to the Platts out near West Roxbury," the boy answered, "but I don't know where he lives. The sheriff said something about him borrowing money to buy a farm and then never paying it back."

"It's not easy to borrow money for a farm," Daniel said. He had heard a lot of hard luck stories down at the boarding house. "Most of the banks won't lend a cent to a farmer because it's so risky."

"Oh, the banks are no use," the boy agreed. "But there's a lot of rich men in Boston willing to lend at high rates. Rich merchants—ministers too. I think it was the old Reverend Hopewell was the complainant for this case. Times are hard. Lots of people are trying to borrow money and most of them are slow paying it back—if they ever do."

So the Hopewells were mixed up in this too. Daniel wondered whether the Mr. Platt out by the Farm was kin to this debtor. If he was, how did he feel about the Hopewells? Daniel thought of the possibilities. Maybe he should go and talk to Platt again. That might get him further than hanging around the courthouse. If he hurried down to the Common he could catch old Gerritson taking the mail out to the Farm and ride along with him.

The ride to the Farm was more comfortable than walking, but it wasn't much faster. The horse ambled down the road as if it didn't care whether if it ever got there. Jonas Gerritson never said a word except for an occasional "Giddap" to the horse, so Daniel had plenty of time to think his own thoughts. Could Abner Platt be angry enough at Winslow Hopewell to kill him? He was the one who accused Rory of the killing. He sure didn't look guilty when he said that. He sounded as though he really believed it. But he was wrong about Rory. Maybe he was covering up for someone. Was this Roger Platt his brother or a cousin or something?

When they reached the path to the Farm, Daniel hopped off the wagon, thanked old Gerritson for the ride and walked toward Platt's place. The house was small and weatherbeaten. The front yard was filled with a vegetable patch; several large pumpkins sprawled across the dirt and some stakes held up browning tomato vines. Dried and broken corn stalks drooped toward the ground. A young boy was throwing kernels of corn on the ground to feed a few skinny brown chickens and a rooster. He stared at Daniel but didn't answer to a cheerful, "Hello there!"

Two men were coming out of the barn carrying spades. When they saw Daniel, one of them turned abruptly and went back in. Daniel called out a greeting to Abner Platt and he walked slowly toward him.

"What are you doing over here, young man?" the farmer asked, his forehead wrinkled with suspicion. "Aren't you supposed to be finding out who killed that young minister over at the Farm?"

"I am working for the *Transcript*, yes, but I wanted to ask you a couple of questions about your brother."

"Which brother would that be? I've got five of them—good hardworking men all of them. What kind of questions are you asking?"

"I was down at the Courthouse today and noticed a broadside notice about a Roger Platt. Would that be one of your brothers?"

"Was if he is? Roger's a good honest man too. Trying to make a living like the rest of us Americans. If it weren't for all the foreigners coming in, we'd be able to do it. And the bankers too! They push a man around when times are bad. There's no justice to it. A man has to feed his family."

"Have you seen your brother lately?"

"None of your business! Now get off my property with all your questions. This farm is mine and there's no one welcome here unless I want them. Tell your newspaper and all the busybodies in the city to tend to their own affairs. We're taking care of our own."

There was no sign of the second man, and Daniel didn't waste time looking for him, but just headed over toward Brook Farm. He was hoping to see Charlotte and tell her all this news. It seemed like they were getting someplace at last. It seemed likely that Roger Platt was hiding out on his brother's farm. He could have run into Winslow Hopewell and gotten into an argument about the debt he owed to his father. Abner Platt made those accusations about Rory to save his brother. Well that hadn't worked. Daniel was feeling pleased with himself as he walked across the road and up the path to the Hive.

Everyone was in the dining room having dinner when he arrived so he stood outside on the porch until he head the them singing. That was a sign the meal was over and time for him to walk around to the kitchen door to find Charlotte. The red-haired student named Fred let him in.

"You're the reporter," he said accusingly. "Are you going to write another story about us? Why don't you write about the great things we are doing here instead of about a tragedy that has nothing to do with us?"

"The sooner people know for certain that no one on the Farm has anything to do with the Reverend Hopewell's death, the better off you'll be. I'm doing my best to find the truth."

Charlotte was still sitting at the table talking to Abigail and another woman. Daniel hovered around the door waiting to talk to her and keeping an eye out for Mr. Ripley, so he could tell him about Abner Platt's brother. Charlotte's hands were fluttering as she talked to Abigail, who sat as still and serene as the Madonna she resembled. The two of them reminded Daniel of a lively wren flitting around a rock dove perched on a cliff. Pretty soon Timothy ran over to his mother and both the women stood up. Abigail went out into the hallway with the boy, and Charlotte walked toward Daniel.

"You look quite satisfied with yourself," she said. "Have you discovered anything new?"

"New and important both. Can we sit in the music room for a few minutes and talk about it or do you have to teach this afternoon?"

"Today is Wednesday, our half holiday. I promised Fanny I'd help her with pickling this afternoon, but we can talk for a little while."

Daniel told her about finding the broadside at the sheriff's office and about his visit to Abner Platt's farm. "Why did the second man run away from me and hide in the barn?" he asked. "That must have been Roger Platt. And if he escaped from the jail three weeks ago, he would have been here when Winslow Hopewell was killed."

"He could have been out early in the morning doing some chores to help his brother and then he sees Reverend Hopewell. He probably recognizes him. After all, he's been borrowing money from Hopewell's father so he's probably familiar with the family."

"But why would he kill Reverend Hopewell even if he did recognize him? It wasn't his fault that Roger couldn't pay his father back. What makes you think the man is a killer?"

"But don't you see how it could happen? Abner Platt is angry at bankers, and I think he'd include anyone who was a moneylender. He was certainly upset about that brother of his who lost his farm in Pennsylvania and now here's another brother who's sent to jail because he can't pay his debts. These are bad times—rock bottom times—farmers like the Platts are angry at anyone who has money. Mr. Cabot says we're likely to have another revolution if times don't get better soon."

"You might be right," Charlotte still hesitated, "but there's no proof of anything."

"That's why we have to get proof. I'm bound and determined to do that. Are you willing to help?

CHAPTER TWELVE

Daniel Tries Spying

October 19, 1842

Daniel and Charlotte walked slowly down the path toward the road thinking their own thoughts. Neither of them knew exactly what had happened, but there were lots of possibilities. It would be natural for a man who broke out of jail to go to his brother's house to hide. And he could have seen Winslow Hopewell and recognized him. But what kind of man would become so angry that he would strike out at an innocent man because of something his father had done? He would have to be a violent and dangerous man.

Charlotte shivered when she thought about it. The sky was gray and filled with threatening clouds making the whole world look threatening. Neither she nor Daniel said anything until they reached the Platt's kitchen yard.

Oliver Platt, the ten-year-old son was in the yard half-heartedly pulling up weeds from the cabbage patch. He watched the two of them approach out of the corner of his eyes. Daniel turned to walk along the road past the Platt's cornfield.

"We can't ask Abner Platt to let us search his house or his barn," he muttered. "Not when he just ordered me off his property. All we can do now is try to find a place where I could watch the house and see who goes in and out. If Roger Platt is staying there, he'll surely come out to help with chores."

"Do you think you could crouch down behind a chokecherry bush?" Charlotte teased him, hoping to lighten the mood. "There aren't even any leaves left on those at this time of year."

"I'm not daft enough to try to spy on them when it's broad daylight. Roger Platt is likely to stay indoors until after dark. I just want to find a place where I could see the house and the path to the barn."

It wasn't easy to find a likely spot. The Platt farm lay in a little depression between the road and the cornfield that rose up on a small hillside the other side of the house. Anyone walking, or even sitting, along the road or beside the cornfield would stand out against the sky, visible to anyone coming out of the house. Aside from a few maple trees alongside the farmhouse, there was no patch of trees closer than the pines behind Brook Farm. Oliver was not even pretending do any weeding now. He was staring straight at the two of them. No doubt he'd tell his father about their behavior—strangers walking slowly along the road looking at the fields.

Finally they found a sheltered spot behind a large rock on the hillside near the cornfield. Daniel said he was going to get some work clothes and a quilt so he'd be able to stay all night and watch the farmyard.

"It would be a waste of time for you to go back to the city to get yourself some clothes," Charlotte pointed out. "I'm sure I can find some at the Farm. Fred would probably lend you his. You're not too different in size."

Fred was willing to lend a pair of trousers and a blue, Brook Farm tunic. He would have liked to join in the spying himself, but the Ripleys were very strict about having the students stay in their rooms at night. Charlotte had to smile when she saw Daniel dressed in Fred's clothes. She'd never seen him before except in a suit and cravat so the blue tunic and farmer's trousers made him look much younger. He couldn't be much older than she was, she realized.

By this time it was getting dark. Charlotte gave Daniel a couple of apples to take with him and an old quilt to wrap around himself as he set off for his hiding place. She was impatient having to stay at the Farm and not tell anyone what was going on, so she settled down to read the book of Mr. Emerson's essays that Mrs. Ripley had recommended. But she couldn't keep her mind on the words. Was Roger Platt really hiding in his brother's farm? What would Daniel do if he saw him? Maybe the man would strike him too. Maybe the man was a cold-hearted murderer. They knew nothing about him. She remembered seeing a mob of farmers protesting back in England. They smashed a thrashing machine their landlord had brought in to replace them. And they attacked the foreman at the farm too and beat him badly. She recalled how he held his hand up to his bleeding face and pleaded, "Let me be! Let me be!"

With those pictures in her mind, she didn't sleep much that night and was up long before dawn. The wind had an edge to it and there was a bit of frost on the ground as she walked carefully over to the Platt farm. Light was just creeping up the horizon and she could barely find her way. She should have had a lantern, but had been afraid to take one for fear the Platts would see her.

Daniel was flung out on the ground with the quilt wrapped round him. He looked fast asleep, but he sat up abruptly when she got close.

"What a sleepyhead!" Charlotte whispered to him. "How do you expect to see Roger Platt if you can't even stay awake?"

"I wasn't asleep," he protested. "Well, maybe I dozed off for a minute. But I swear there was no one going into or out of the house or barn last night."

It was very quiet, but dawn was creeping up the sky. The roosters would be crowing soon—and sure enough there was one now. Then the cows started lowing and they heard a dog give a sleepy bark.

"What do we do now?" Charlotte whispered to Daniel. "Are you sure you saw someone last night? Maybe his brother is staying in the house with the family. Maybe it's a different brother and not the one who broke out of jail at all."

Just then the back door to the house opened. They saw Abner Platt coming out wearing a plaid jacket and a shabby hat and carrying a small lantern. Soon he disappeared into the barn leaving the door open behind him. They could see him moving around the barn in the lantern light milking the cows.

"You'd think if he was hiding his brother, there would be two of them working," whispered Charlotte. But just then the back door opened again and a second man came out and walked toward the barn. Daniel had been right. Someone was staying with the Platts.

"I'm going to speak to him," said Daniel. He stood up and moved toward the barn.

"You can't go looking like you spent the night sleeping in a field," Charlotte protested. "The Platts will think you're another Irish tramp like Rory. Why don't you change your clothes and come back when you can persuade them you're from the newspaper?"

Reluctantly he agreed and they walked back to Brook Farm where people were just beginning to get up and start on the day. Daniel went off to talk to Fred and find his own clothes while Charlotte helped the breakfast team set the table for breakfast. When Daniel came to the kitchen with Fred, Mrs. Geary took one look at him and offered to give him something to eat.

It was an hour or more before the meal was finished and dishes cleaned away. Daniel and Charlotte finally got away and walked back to see the Platts. This time Daniel looked like a real gentleman in a suit, carrying sheets of paper to write notes on. With his dark hair blowing into his forehead from the wind, he looked both handsome and strong. She was afraid he might have to be strong if Abner and Roger Platt caused any trouble.

This time they knocked on the front door of the farmhouse. A plump, red-faced woman opened it for us. She looked surprised, but she must have recognized Charlotte because she said "You are from Brook Farm, aren't you? What is it you want with us?"

"We'd like to speak to your husband," said Daniel. He stepped into the kitchen and Charlotte followed him. Abner Platt was sitting at a wooden table with Oliver and a younger child they hadn't seen before. Abner Platt stood up when he saw them.

"You're that young reporter who's been nosing around the Ripley's place, aren't you?" he asked. "Didn't I tell you yesterday to stay off my property?"

"We have reason to believe you are harboring a wanted man," Daniel pulled out the broadsheet with the information about Roger

Platt. "He has been seen lurking around your farm. Are you telling me he isn't here?"

"Don't you threaten me, young man!" the farmer shook his fist at Daniel as he spoke. "My family's been farming here for four generations and we don't have to answer to the likes of you. You can go back where you come from and leave us honest folks alone. That broadsheet ain't worth the paper it's printed on. My brother will be cleared of all charges and free by the end of the day. Now get off my property. I don't want to see your face around here again."

It was impossible to talk to such an angry man, but Daniel wasn't about to give up the fight. They walked slowly back to Brook Farm where the early morning work in the barn was still going on. Mr. Ripley was walking back toward the house carrying two pails of milk. He looked puzzled when he saw them.

"Excuse me, sir," Daniel said to him. "Miss Edgerton and I have discovered something that might give us more information about the Reverend Hopewell's death. Could we speak with you for a few minutes?"

George Ripley left the milk in on the porch and led them into his small office. Books were stacked on the floor around the walls and two ladder-backed chairs faced the bare table that served as his desk. How could one man have so many books? Charlotte knew that all the bookshelves lining the hallway outside were filled with Ripley's books too.

"I don't have much time, young man," Mr. Ripley began, peering through his wire-rimmed spectacles. "The sheriff is investigating Reverend Hopewell's death and I don't believe a reporter should meddle with his work."

For a moment Daniel looked taken aback, so Charlotte jumped in, "The sheriff has a great deal on his mind and many calls on his time. Mr. Gallagher is trying to help find the facts quickly so our Community does not suffer from the scandal."

By this time Daniel was his usual brash self and he continued, "Some information fell into my hands about Mr. Platt's brother, Roger Platt. Did you know that he had been in debtor's prison for the last two months? Furthermore the debt he owed was to Thomas Hopewell, father of Reverend Hopewell. Just three weeks ago Roger Platt broke out of the jail. The sheriff is looking for him now, but I believe I know where he is."

George Ripley's eyebrows rose above his glasses and he looked skeptically at Daniel, who hurried on. "Last night I saw a strange man lurking around the Platt's place and I believe that is Roger Platt. When Charlotte and I asked about him, Abner Platt refused to tell us anything. He chased us off his farm."

"Well, he did tell us something," Charlotte broke in. "He told us his brother would be cleared of all charges and that the broadside was a mistake."

"Can you believe that?" demanded Daniel. "There's no way he could repay the money if he was in jail. But the important thing is he was free when Reverend Hopewell was killed—and he was hiding just across the road from where the crime was committed."

.

CHAPTER THIRTEEN

Daniel Solves a Puzzle

October 20, 1842

After the talk with George Ripley, Charlotte had to go back to her classes. Fanny was hovering outside the office door and she scowled as she complained to Charlotte, "Do you think I can take care of all the children? I have enough work with the infants and no time to teach letters to your primary group. We are all supposed to share work here."

"Yes, I know," returned Charlotte meekly. "I did not mean to leave you with my class so long. Thank you very much for your help." She nodded briefly to Daniel and left.

Daniel started on the long, weary walk back to Boston pondering what he should do to convince George Ripley and the others that Roger Platt might be dangerous. The answer to questions about Roger Platt's debt and his time in jail could only come from the sheriff. As he walked Daniel sketched out in his mind the sequence of events. Roger Platt had borrowed money from Reverend Thomas Hopewell who, as everyone knew, was a rich man and a fairly generous one too. Banks weren't lending any money these days, but a man who held title to a farm could find private money.

When Roger couldn't pay his debt, Hopewell grew impatient. He must have petitioned the court and the sheriff wasted no time sending Roger to jail. Small hope of his repaying the debt from there while his wife was probably struggling to keep the farm going. Many a man would be desperate enough to break out of jail if he could. It happened all the time. What would be more natural than for him to turn to his brother to hide until it was safe for him to go back home? But what was this talk about his being cleared? How could that happen? Then Daniel realized. The man he had to see was Thomas Hopewell, not the sheriff.

First he would stop at the boarding house and get some fresh clothes. Maybe even take a nap. He certainly hadn't had much sleep the night before. No one could sleep crouched on that rocky hillside watching the Platt's farm. When he reached the boarding house, he must have looked as tired and hungry as he felt because Mrs. Costello, his landlady, offered to make tea and she gave him a thick slice of bread and butter to go with it. When he went up to his small attic room, he threw himself on the bed and was asleep in no time.

Next thing he knew, he woke to growing darkness. Time to head toward Beacon Hill. Putting on his best suit, he headed out. The newfangled gas lights were just being lit on the street where Hopewell lived, lighting the way for the prosperous people who lived there. Someday, Daniel swore to himself, he'd live on a street with gas lights. Houses on this block were tall gray buildings that looked as though they would stand for years; quite a contrast to Daniel's neighborhood of ramshackle wooden buildings. The massive First Unitarian Church loomed over the houses and next to it the minister's manse where the Reverend Hopewell lived.

Daniel knocked on the door, using the large brass knocker that had been wrapped in black cloth as a mark of mourning. It gave a muffled thump and he waited patiently for a response. Finally an elderly woman with a thin, bony face came to the door, a housekeeper he judged by her dull black dress and white apron.

"What do you want, young man?" she asked in a clipped New England voice narrowing her eyes suspiciously.

"I would like to talk with Reverend Hopewell. I have some information concerning his son's death that might be useful to him."

"Humph!" she exclaimed, looking him up and down. "Reverend Hopewell is mourning. He has a great deal on his mind and better things to do than listen to an idle stranger."

"Would you please ask him if I could talk to him?" Daniel persisted. "I have just been visiting Brook Farm and I believe he might be interested in what I have to tell him."

"Step inside then and I'll see whether he wants to speak to you," she said, opening the door just wide enough for him to squeeze through.

She soon came back and without saying anything beckoned him to follow her. The room she led him to had rows of bookshelves around the walls and a large fire blazing in the fireplace. A white-haired man wearing a black velvet morning jacket and a tasseled cap was seated in a dark green wingback chair so large that it dwarfed his shrunken body. He was thin and looked rather frail, but his gray eyes were sharp. Daniel stood awkwardly in front of him.

"What do you have to tell me?" Reverend Hopewell asked in a clear authoritative voice.

"I have discovered that a man to whom you lent money, a man who recently escaped from debtor's jail, was hiding just across the road from Brook Farm when your son was there. I thought you should know that this fugitive, who might have had some reason for quarreling with your family, possibly even threatening them, was close by when your son was attacked."

For a long minute the man said nothing. Then he gestured to Daniel, "Sit down, sit down" waving him to the wingback chair on the other side of the fireplace. "Tell me who you are and what you know about my son."

Daniel introduced himself and continued his story, "His name is Roger Platt. I believe you signed a complaint against him for unpaid debts. His brother Abner's farm is just across the road from Brook Farm. I believe he has been hiding at his brother's place. Perhaps when he heard your son was visiting Brook Farm his anger at you was transferred to your family. When he saw your son taking a walk that morning, he could have gone over to ask him to intercede with you to give him more time to pay his debt. If your son quarreled with him that could have led to the terrible attack."

"You have that story half right, young man. He did see my son at Brook Farm and he did ask for help with the debt, but there was no quarrel. No need for a struggle." The old man leaned one elbow on the arm of his chair and bent his head to his hand. His shoulders shook with silent sobs for a moment, but he soon controlled himself and continued.

"My son was a very generous man. Far more generous than I am, I'm afraid. When he heard Roger Platt's story, he wrote to our lawyer and paid the debt with his own money. By the time I heard about it my son was already..." his voice wavered, "my son was gone. It was only two days ago I informed the sheriff that the charges should be dropped."

Daniel was left speechless. "Your son certainly was a very generous man," he finally said to the grieving father. "You must have been very proud of him."

"I was proud of him, although I seldom told him so. I chided him for being frivolous and not marrying a sensible woman. He was too flattered by the idle matrons in his congregation, women who had husbands and children they should have attended to instead of trifling with the time of their minister."

Thomas Hopewell continued talking, scarcely looking at Daniel, as though it was a relief to pour out his thoughts, "He paid little attention to some very suitable young women, any one of whom would have made him a good wife and borne him children to inherit his gifts and his name. The only young woman he ever seemed to care about was that young Quaker girl years ago, but of course he could not marry a Quaker. We quarreled over that.

"We quarreled over many things and I was often angry with him. But I should have told him how proud I was of all the good he did despite his faults. He was planning to invest money in George Ripley's community. That must have been the money he used to pay Roger Platt's debt."

The old man fell silent, and when he spoke again his voice was very soft and sounded less certain than it had. "God has been hard on me. He took my wife and daughter. Winslow was all I had left and now he is gone too. But we must bear God's will patiently. He tests us only for our own good." The Reverend Hopewell's voice grew stronger as he spoke. He would survive his pain to give many more sermons to his flock.

Night had fallen when Daniel left the house. He felt far less certain about anything than he had when he went there. He had been sure that he had solved the mystery of Winslow Hopewell's death. Now he was certain of nothing.

CHAPTER FOURTEEN

Abigail Has a Holiday

October 23, 1842.

Sunday brought a bright, crisp day that tempted everyone outdoors. Pumpkins were ripening in the vegetable patch and the younger Brook Farmers were determined to decorate them and celebrate Halloween. George Ripley didn't altogether approve of such a heathenish holiday, but he did not forbid the frolicking.

Although the students planned the festival, many adults quickly joined in. John Dwight promised to play his flute for dancing in the pine grove. After Sunday dinner Fred and Lloyd invited everyone in the dining room to walk out to the pine grove and share an afternoon dance and picnic. Costumes would be welcome but were not necessary. Timothy begged his mother to share in the fun. There seemed no harm in it even though Abigail was sure her Quaker ancestors would have been shocked if they had known she allowed her son to take part in such a pagan rite. She breathed an apology to them as she prepared to enjoy the holiday.

Ever since Winslow had died in the midst of trees Abigail had been reluctant to walk among any trees. He had been at some distance from the pine grove, but the sight of the dark pine trees in the woods recalled him to mind. She struggled against the feeling, knowing that grieving too long was a sin, and that she should welcome the happiness to be found in God's world and its beauties. It was time for joy to return to Brook Farm, especially for the sake of the children. But joy was hard to find at Brook Farm right now, Abigail thought. She shivered as she looked around the woods and thought about how someone had intruded on their peaceful pleasures and brought such misery. Perhaps some of the evil spirits of Halloween really did haunt these woods.

Charlotte, Ellen and Abigail joined the procession walking to the grove. Some of the girls had woven autumn leaves into their hair, although there were few of the colorful leaves left. Ellen had found Queen Anne's Lace and made a little nosegay of it for her dress; it gleamed, white and lacy against the dark blue fabric.

Even Mrs. Geary came along, looking more cheerful than she usually did. She seldom joined in festivities, but Halloween was an Irish holiday that recalled memories of her youth. She was going to help the children pick pumpkins and carve them into faces. As they walked she told the others that she usually made colcannon for Halloween dinner, a mixture of mashed potatoes and cabbage. She said mischievously, "The most important part of it is to bury a coin in the bowl. Whoever gets the coin in his portion is destined to have a prosperous year ahead."

"Not too many of us have found that coin, it seems," said Ellen. "When was the last time any Irishman was prosperous?"

Her mother sighed and remarked, "We take what the Lord gives us and make the best of it."

Soon the sound of music from the grove cheered everyone. Some of the boys were singing a popular college song:

We'll sing tonight with hearts as light

And joys as gay and fleeting

As bubbles that swim on the beaker's brim

And break on the lips at meeting.

John Dwight had gathered some of his students to form a choir and sing ballads as they sat on the rocks or on the bed of pine needles on the ground. One of the students took out a fiddle and began to play dance music. Even Timothy wanted to join in that, so Abigail took him by the hands and led him in a whirl around the grove to the strains of "Bonny Lassey". For the first time in weeks everyone was smiling and enjoying themselves. Red-headed Fred was trying to follow Ellen who was showing him how to dance an Irish jig. Poor Fred screwed his forehead in concentration while Ellen's feet moved so fast he could scarcely follow her steps.

When Timothy grew tired of dancing and moved off to collect pine cones with Johnny Parsons. Abigail sat down on a rock next to Fanny Gray. Even Fanny was not looking cross today. Abigail asked her whether she was enjoying the sunny weather.

"Oh, indeed I am enjoying it," she answered. "This morning I walked over to Dedham to hear Theodore Parker's sermon. He talked about the evil of slavery in the South and how all Christians should resist efforts to allow it to spread. He fortified my spirit with his brave ideas."

"I agree that we must end the evil of slavery, but the slave states are so far away from us. Men can make speeches and vote to change the laws, but what can we women do about the evil of slavery?"

Fanny leaned toward her and spoke in a soft voice as she replied, "Don't you understand there are activities going on right under our noses?" She leaned so close Abigail could smell cinnamon on her breath, and her eyes looked huge. "My friend Tabitha has told me about many things that are going on in Massachusetts, some of them as close as Boston. There are escape routes from the South that lead straight through this area. Many runaways travel by ship to Boston and then follow the rivers north to Montreal. There are safe houses along the way where they can shelter."

Abigail had heard nothing of this in Massachusetts. In Philadelphia she had overheard talk about runaway slaves among the Quakers. Some of them had felt the call to work with the Underground Railway and help slaves flee cruel masters in the South. Boston seemed far away from that, although the newspapers were filled with arguments being made about new laws for the new states.

"That must be dangerous," Abigail finally said. Even to herself she sounded like a coward as she said it.

Fanny drew back and looked at her sternly. "Of course it is dangerous, but sometimes we have to accept danger. We have to be strong and willing to raise our hands against people who are doing evil." Her face was becoming quite red with the strength of her emotion.

The wind was getting quite chilly and when Sophia Ripley suggested they start walking back to the Hive, Abigail was happy to go. Charlotte joined them and they slowly meandered back through the wood and across the brown meadow toward the building.

Sophia Ripley talked about Winslow. "He was such a promising young man," she said. "Do you know that he was being considered for a call to become the chief minister at the First Unitarian Church in Salem? He spoke to me about that once."

"It would have been a great honor for him," Abigail said. He had not mentioned that to her. So many dreams had died that day. "Salem would have been a perfect opportunity for him."

"Yes," agreed Sophia, "but he was troubled by something. He talked to me one evening about whether I thought a man should reveal all of his sins, every shameful deed he had ever done, to the congregation before he accepted a new pulpit."

"Did Reverend Hopewell have any shameful secrets?" asked Fanny doubtfully. "He was a respected clergyman just as his father is. No one ever suggested he had shameful secrets, although he was not always a man to keep his promises. I don't believe he even thought that was shameful."

"Do you mean his promise to invest in our Community?" Sophia asked gently. "Surely he was not speaking of that. That is a business affair, which he discussed with my husband. He would not have talked to me about money matters."

"Well, I don't understand what else he could have been ashamed of," Fanny persisted, frowning now.

Abigail was busy trying to understand what Winslow could have meant. Did he think it had been a sin for the two of them to have a Quaker wedding? Could he have meant he was ashamed of having denied the wedding afterward? But Sophia had more to say.

"He mentioned that some people liked to reveal the private affairs of others and that it would be terrible for a minister if anyone decided to uncover all the mistakes of youth. He said he regretted some of his youthful actions, but he never told me more than that."

Charlotte pondered this. "It sounds as though he was afraid of having his secret revealed. Perhaps it wasn't that he felt guilty, but more that he was afraid of someone who knew his secret."

Sophia Ripley frowned incredulously, "Do you mean that someone was threatening him? Surely Reverend Hopewell was not afraid of blackmail!"

Blackmail was such an ugly word. It was not a word any of them would connect with Winslow Hopewell. Surely no one would dare to threaten him. No one had any answer for Sophia, so the four of them continued walking to the Hive in silence.

CHAPTER FIFTEEN

Daniel Asks Questions

October 24, 1842.

The conversation with Thomas Hopewell left Daniel discouraged. He had been certain Roger Platt must be the killer. Writing the story as an exclusive for the *Transcript* would most likely get him a permanent job with the newspaper. He could almost hear Mr. Cabot's congratulations, and he smiled to think that Charlotte would look at him with a bit more respect. It would be a pleasure to impress a clever girl like Charlotte Edgerton. Instead he found himself walking back to the boarding house in the dark on a cold, rainy night no further ahead than he'd been the night before.

He stopped in a tavern for a plate of fried kidneys and a pint of ale, but they didn't help much. If the Platts had no reason to kill Winslow Hopewell, who would have? He was a respected man, a preacher and a friend of the Ripleys. His watch and his money weren't stolen. It made no sense. Hopewell wasn't a fighting man or a political man as far as Daniel knew. Who could have hated him enough to kill him? With a sigh Daniel turned toward his boarding house. By the time he got there the door was locked and Mrs. Costello grumbled when she opened it. "I keep a respectable house, young man. If you want to spend your nights drinking you can find another landlady."

"Sure I'd never find one as lovely as you," Daniel answered, trying to smooth her furrowed brow. "You remind me of my sainted grandmother in heaven. You wouldn't want to turn me away from my better angels, would you?" That made her smile and he ran upstairs before she could say anything else.

On Sunday morning Daniel went to mass hoping to run into Rory O'Connor. Could Rory tell him anything more about what had happened that morning? Well, wherever Rory was, he wasn't in church. Daniel plodded back to the boarding house for breakfast and spent most of the afternoon reading the books he had borrowed from Miss Peabody's bookstore. Questions about Winslow's death nagged at him. Who could have wanted him dead? Who could have been lurking around Brook Farm? Could it have been an accident? But there were no answers.

On Monday morning Daniel made up his mind to talk to the sheriff again. Maybe there were leads that were being followed. When he got to the Court House, Sheriff Grover was in his office and the same clerk in the same black suit was sitting in a corner copying documents. The sheriff recognized Daniel, but he didn't look very happy about it.

"You're that reporter from the *Transcript*, eh? What do you want this time? Have you found another body? Or have those folks at Brook Farm gotten into some other kind of mischief?"

"Nothing like that, sir. I was just wondering whether the investigation into Reverend Hopewell's murder was still going on. Perhaps you already know who the culprit is? The citizens of Boston would like to know that such an evildoer had been captured."

"We are not miracle workers. We can't solve crimes when there are no clues and no criminals in the neighborhood to question. Perhaps Winslow Hopewell fell and hit his head. Likely it was a death by misadventure. That's the verdict I will recommend to the coroner when he holds a hearing on the matter."

That decision startled Daniel and he protested. "How do you explain the mark of a blow on his forehead?" he asked.

"He could have fallen on a rock or a hoe or rake. Perhaps he was carrying one. At any rate I am not going to keep bothering those good people at Brook Farm and I certainly don't want to cause a scandal for the Reverend Thomas Hopewell. The Hopewells are one of the leading families of the county, of the entire Commonwealth of Massachusetts."

Daniel could see the way the land lay. No official in Boston was going to cause a scandal to one of the leading families no matter how many crimes were committed. But he wasn't satisfied to stand by and see the murder denied that way. A man should be allowed to live out his life and from what Thomas Hopewell had told him, it seemed that Winslow was a man whose life was doing some good in the world. Wasn't America supposed to be a land of justice? Keeping the gentry out of trouble was acting like the corrupt officials in Ireland. It wasn't supposed to happen in this new country. No use saying that to the sheriff though.

Time for another trip to Brook Farm. That's where the crime had happened, so that must be the place that held the answer. Daniel had to find a solution. He wasn't fooling himself that it was all for lofty ideas about justice either. Solving the mystery would be the key to a new job and a place of importance in the city. He had spent enough years scrabbling around to make a living. It was time to have a suitable place in the world and maybe settle down.

The weather had changed again; gray rainclouds were gathering along the Western horizon and a sharp wind was blowing them in fast. Crinkled brown leaves swirled along the edge of the road and teased at his ankles. There would be frost tonight.

Once again Daniel arrived at the Farm while everyone was in at their dinner. He went round to the kitchen door where Mrs. Geary smiled when she saw him. She cut him a slice of pork roast and gave him some baked beans to go with it. It was the best meal he'd eaten in a long time and sharing a table with her made it easy to talk. He had never heard her say anything about why she and Ellen lived at Brook Farm or what she thought of the people here. He had been a child when she left Galway with her new husband and he hadn't paid much attention to why they were going. Today, without his even asking, she started talking about how she and Ellen had come to Brook Farm.

"My husband wanted more than anything to get an education for his children," she said. "He never went to school at all, any more than I did, but the priest taught him to read and write and he learned everything so quickly it was astonishing. His father wanted to make him a priest, but he and I had found each other when we were young and we were determined to have our own lives. Patrick saved up every penny he earned on the fishing boats to buy us passage to America. My parents were willing to let me go, and so the priest called the banns and we were married the day before the ship sailed. Patrick's father never forgave him for leaving, but he softened a bit after Ellen was born and sent a letter with his blessing for all of us.

"Oh, it's too long a story to tell you. We struggled in Boston. Patrick never could get a job anywhere except on the docks. He wanted to be a clerk, and his writing was beautiful, but no one would hire an Irishman for that, so he worked on the docks until it killed him. His lungs were never strong and one winter he just got so sick he couldn't get out of bed. Finally God took him. His last wish was that Ellen could go to school, so I promised him I'd do that no matter what. She was already quite a scholar because he taught her all the reading and writing he knew. I worked as a kitchen maid for Mrs. Ripley, and when she and Reverend Ripley started Brook Farm they were willing to take me as a cook. They promised Ellen could go to school here and so she has."

By this time dinner was over and people were bringing the plates and tableware out to the kitchen to wash. Charlotte was surprised to find Daniel chatting with Mrs. Geary.

"It's nice to see you," she said. "I've something to tell you but not until after I've given my class their afternoon lessons. It won't be too long and you can help wash up the dishes and clean the kitchen to pay for your dinner."

She laughed when she said that and went off quickly to gather her class together. Daniel was just as happy to stay and work with the cleaning group in the kitchen. They sang while they washed the dishes. Fred was very interested in working on a newspaper and while he and Daniel dried the dishes they had plenty to talk about.

Finally Charlotte came down from her classroom after having delivered her students back to their parents. She and Daniel found a quiet corner of the parlor. He told her about visiting Thomas Hopewell and what he had said about his son paying Roger's debt.

"I was sure we had found the murderer when we learned that Roger had escaped from debtor's prison," Daniel admitted. "But by the time Winslow Hopewell died, Roger must have known that the debt was paid. He was just staying with his brother until the judge had officially freed him. Now I don't know where to look for another suspect."

"You're not the only one who learned something new," Charlotte said. "Yesterday I was talking with Mrs. Ripley and she told me Reverend Hopewell was very troubled these past weeks. He was being considered for a new position as minister at the largest church in Salem."

"He must have been pleased by that," Daniel said. "He was an ambitious man I'm sure."

"But he was troubled. Mrs. Ripley said he talked about a secret and how he was afraid someone might learn about it. He talked about mistakes made in youth that come back to haunt a man."

"Youthful mistakes!" Daniel echoed. "Do you think he was afraid someone would reveal them and then he wouldn't be offered the position? Someone was blackmailing him, was that it?"

Charlotte seemed to consider this for a minute. "I think that might have been the trouble. There was something he didn't want told to the congregation. He thought they would disapprove."

"We have to find out what these youthful indiscretions were." It was hard to believe that Reverend Hopewell, who was always described as almost perfect, could have had a guilty secret. "We need to find out what he did that he was ashamed of. And especially who it was who knew his secret."

Charlotte gave him a strange, strained look. She was twisting a handkerchief in her hands as she spoke, but she stopped talking and stared absently at the bookcase for a few minutes. Finally she said in a very quiet voice, "I've heard something else too, something I promised not to tell anyone, but perhaps it's important. Perhaps I have to tell you." She stopped talking and sat very still.

"If it helps us find out who killed Winslow Hopewell, don't you think you'd better tell me?"

"Yes, I suppose I should. You see, I know what his secret was. And I know the person who knows about it."

Charlotte Visits a Bookstore

October 24, 1842.

The parlor was deserted except for two of the younger students sprawled on the floor reading a book of Greek myths and whispering together. Charlotte drew in her breath and decided she had to tell Daniel about Abigail's secret even though it felt like a betrayal. Her throat was tight when she started talking and she glanced over her shoulder to make sure the students weren't close enough to hear anything.

"Abigail and Winslow Hopewell knew each other very well," she started "because the Hopewells were friends of the aunt that Abigail lived with in Boston and they used to visit the house. Winslow Hopewell came very often. He told Abigail he wanted to marry her, but he was afraid his father would be very angry. He was supposed to become a minister like his father, and marrying a Quaker was not something a minister should do. I guess they are too radical for respectable Unitarians."

"You know it's strange," Daniel added when she paused, "Reverend Thomas Hopewell mentioned that his son had once liked a

Quaker girl. He said that of course marrying a Quaker was impossible. I suppose he must have been talking about Abigail."

"That must be it," Charlotte agreed. "I don't know whether Winslow actually told his father he wanted to marry Abigail, or whether the father just suspected it. Anyway, the two of them decided—I guess it was Abigail who suggested it—that they would have a Quaker wedding. Did you know that Quakers don't get married in a church? They just declare to each other, usually in front of other people I guess, that they are married and then they are.

"I don't know whether Abigail ever told her aunt about it, but she and Winslow Hopewell—he wasn't a Reverend then—considered themselves man and wife. At least Abigail believed that. Then, after he became a minister, Reverend Winslow Hopewell must have decided he couldn't continue having a secret marriage. He told Abigail he didn't believe they were really married. And he went off to serve as an assistant minister in a church up in Portland and Abigail never saw him again until he came to the Farm."

"So that was his guilty secret?" Daniel muttered thoughtfully. "Do you think he would have been rejected for this new post if people knew he once had a secret marriage?"

"There's more," Charlotte continued. "Reverend Hopewell was Timothy's father, although he never knew that until just a few weeks ago. Timothy was born after his father had gone to Portland and Abigail never told him about the baby."

"But what about this Mr. Pretlove that Abigail was married to?"

"There was no one named Pretlove. Abigail pretended she was a widow because she had to explain having Timothy. Her aunt helped her and told everyone the widow story. I guess no one suggested it wasn't true. I think maybe the two of them moved to Salem or someplace where no one knew them."

"That puts a different light on it," exclaimed Daniel. "No church would want a minister who had a bastard son." His cheeks flushed scarlet. "Begging your pardon, I shouldn't have used such language in front of you."

"I'm not a dainty lady like some of the people here, you know," Charlotte retorted. "My father and mother were plain-spoken people who weren't afraid to call something by its name. But if the two of them were married that makes a difference, doesn't it?"

"Would the wedding be legal if no one saw it and it wasn't recorded at the courthouse?" Daniel wondered aloud. Neither of them knew the answer to that. Then he asked the question that had been bothering Charlotte. "Was Mrs. Pretlove very angry at Reverend Hopewell? You don't suppose they could have quarreled and then maybe she hit him and..." his voice dwindled away.

"She couldn't have killed him. She never would have done that." Charlotte's voice sounded angry although she was trying to be very calm. The thought of anyone suspecting Abigail made her wretched, even though a little doubt kept wriggling into her mind.

"No, I don't think she could have" Daniel agreed, "but who else would have known the story and perhaps threatened him? That's what we have to find out."

"We ought to find out whether Quaker weddings are legal in Massachusetts," Charlotte added. "If they are and Reverend Hopewell knew it, at least he couldn't be blackmailed about Timothy. He still has a lot to be ashamed of. It was cruel to go off and leave Abigail no matter how much he wanted to be a minister like his father."

"If he had been a real man he would have stood up to his father. No one should leave a girl like that. That's cruel and sinful too. Sure I don't think much of a man who hides behind his father's anger as an excuse to philander."

They had had the parlor to themselves for almost an hour, but now Fanny Gray come bustling it. She looked at Daniel with a little frown, "You've been spending a great deal of time here, Mr. Gallagher. Have you been thinking of joining us? A fine, strong-looking man like you would be an asset on the Farm. Have you ever been a farmer?"

Daniel looked a bit alarmed at the suggestion. "No, ma'am, I never have, although I did work a bit on my father's patch of land back in Ireland. But my father was a schoolteacher and something of a poet, not a farmer at all."

"You're young and strong, you could be a great help on the Farm," Fanny insisted. "And if you've planted and harvested vegetables we could use your strong arms. I'm going out to hoe the pumpkin patch myself this afternoon. There aren't a great many vegetables left, but there will be a few still coming in. Think about it. We are starting a whole new plan of life here. You can help with the farm work and have time for your poetry and newspaper writing too."

Daniel stood up and said politely, "I will certainly think about joining your community. I can see that you are doing great things here and perhaps you really will change the world. But I must be leaving now to get back to Boston."

As Daniel turned to leave, Charlotte told him, "I'm going to Miss Peabody's bookstore on Wednesday afternoon. Perhaps I can find out more about these Quaker weddings and what they mean."

On Tuesday there was a slow rain all day, but Wednesday came in bright, clear, and chilly. Charlotte was able to get a ride into Boston on Jonas Gerritson's wagon and was at Miss Peabody's shop early in the afternoon. The shelves looked more crowded than ever with books of every size, some in leather bindings and some in paper. She searched first for the section on religion. That didn't look very promising. Volume after volume of collected sermons and books with titles like *A Christian Liturgy* and *German Writings on the New Testament*—those certainly wouldn't tell anything about Quakers and the law. She sighed with irritation because nothing looked promising.

"You sound discouraged," said a quiet voice behind her. Charlotte whirled around and saw Margaret Fuller. She was examining the books through her lorgnette. "What was it you were looking for?"

"I am looking for a book that would tell me more about Quakers and how they are different from other people. I've never known any Quakers except for Abigail Pretlove at the Farm and I don't know much about their rules and customs."

"You can ask Miss Peabody whether she has any Quaker books, but I rather doubt it. Most of the books on religion here are about Biblical scholarship and quarrels between Unitarian ministers about the nature of God. Perhaps you should go to the New Thinkers Convention next Saturday and Sunday in Dedham. Representatives from most of the newer or more radical groups will be there and I wouldn't be surprised if some Quakers attend."

The bell on the bookshop door jingled as someone came in; it was Daniel, looking very serious and wearing a bright green cravat. He smiled and walked over to join Charlotte. Miss Fuller remembered him, "You are the young reporter who listened to my talk at Brook Farm last week, aren't you? Did you find the talk of interest?"

"It was of great interest indeed. It is very gratifying to hear someone as important as yourself say such kind words about those of us who came to this country from Ireland." Daniel sounded very much like a gentleman despite his brogue.

Charlotte told him quickly about Miss Fuller's suggestion, but he looked doubtful.

"Perhaps this meeting is similar to the one held at the First Church in Dedham last April?" he asked. "I went to one of those meetings and was startled at the people there. Although the meeting was almost over when I arrived, the pews were still half filled with an odd assortment of people. The man who was speaking from the pulpit wore a long white robe spotted with mud from the street. His hair was long and untidy, a wild brush of gray which became more untidy as he ran his hands through it. He was shouting in a loud harsh voice and I remember his words very well: 'Cease your worrying about wealth. Turn to the Lord! Our time is not long. The world will end in 1843 as has been prophesied. Why worry about slavery or economic woes? Our time is running out.' That was enough for me and I turned and left. I have many hopes and fears for the future, but having the world end next year is not one of them." Daniel's face was wreathed in a smile.

Margaret Fuller smiled too. "Some of our so-called 'New Thinkers' have odd thoughts to be sure, but there are others who are concerned about the future have far more sensible plans. The Quakers, for example, differ from most of us in many ways but they are no longer fanatical as they used to be and they have been of great benefit to many in our society."

"Well, perhaps it would be worthwhile to go to the convention," Daniel agreed. "Would you have any intention of going yourself, Miss Fuller?"

"No, I think not," she answered, "although many interested people might attend. I believe that Ralph Emerson attended the one in April and your George Ripley was there too."

"Was Winslow Hopewell at this meeting?" Charlotte asked eagerly.

"I had not heard of his going. He may be conservative like his father. Thomas Hopewell has not welcomed new ideas and plans. That is why I was surprised that his son became interested in Brook Farm. Perhaps he was more accepting than his father of the idea that Boston has not reached perfection yet and that there is some sense in trying new plans of organizing society."

After Miss Fuller left, Daniel and Charlotte asked Miss Peabody about books about Quakers, but the only Quaker book in the store was George Fox's Book of Martyrs, which told nothing about New England. But when she heard that Daniel and Charlotte were especially interested in Quaker weddings, Miss Peabody chattered on about the great controversy these weddings had caused. Only recently had people in Boston started to consider them real weddings. There were still some churches that would not accept a marriage as valid unless it was performed by a minister in a church.

Daniel and Charlotte decided they would walk out to Dedham on Saturday to see whether what there was to learn about Winslow Hopewell and what people thought about him. If his father and his friends thought that participating in a Quaker wedding was a sin, it was no wonder he considered his marriage to Abigail a guilty secret.

CHAPTER SEVENTEEN

Charlotte Gets Unexpected News

October 29, 1842.

Saturday dawned bright but cold. Charlotte had asked Ellen and Fred to go to the meeting at Dedham but only Fred went with her. He was always ready for a trip and the more unusual the meeting, the more he looked forward to it. At the last minute Fanny Gray decided to join them. She often went to the church in Dedham.

    Charlotte wore her stoutest boots and warmest cloak, a red plaid woolen one with a fur-trimmed hood and Fred was bundled up in his heaviest jacket and on his head a warm toque his mother had knit for him. It wasn't a day for the light blue tunic he had been wearing just a few weeks ago. Winter had come with a vengeance, and although they still hadn't had a snowstorm, they were chilly even in their warm clothes. Fred starting singing to cheer everyone us up:

    Cape Cod girls ain't got no combs,

    Heave away, haul away!

    They comb their hair with a codfish bone,

    And we're bound away for Australia!

Cape Cod boys ain't got no sleds,
Heave away, haul away!
They ride down hills on a codfish head.
And we're bound away for Australia!

The wind was still cold, but singing a silly song made everyone feel better. Even Fanny had to smile; Fred's pleasure was contagious. As the sun rose higher in the sky the wind didn't feel so harsh and the walk became almost enjoyable. By the time they had reached Dedham everyone's cheeks and noses were red and their chins were numb from the cold.

The First Church of Dedham was a gray stone building with sparse strands of withered ivy clinging to its walls. It stood in a small churchyard close to the road and two oak trees overhung the burial plot where the gravestones clustered in family plots. A sign outside the door announced the "Convention on New Thinking for Universal Reform" and several people were walking toward the door. Fanny soon joined a group of friends and Fred and Charlotte stepped inside the church. Almost immediately they saw Daniel.

"The first speaker will begin in about half an hour," he told them. "Everyone here has been friendly to me, but I haven't found any Quakers yet. I am not sure how much we will learn."

People were milling around at the back of the church, drawing together in small groups to talk and then separating and moving on. Most of the participants were men, but there were several women, some with their husbands and others on their own. Fanny sat with an elderly woman wearing a black shawl. The two of them were soon whispering together in a back pew while they waited for the talks to begin.

Fred wandered off to talk to some young boys he knew and Daniel and Charlotte introduced themselves to a thin, pale young man with a flowing black cravat and a chestnut-colored jacket who was one of the youngest-looking men there,. He looked at Charlotte approvingly when she said she was a teacher at Brook Farm.

"Oh, I deeply admire George Ripley's innovation with that community," he drawled. "Sometimes I think of joining the group myself, but alas I am a poet and when the inspiration comes to me I must seize it and write. I cannot afford to be distracted by details such as a cow that needs milking or wheat to harvest. My friend Nathaniel Hawthorne tried living at Ripley's Farm, but farm work interfered with the flow of his thoughts."

"Yes, I had heard that Mr. Hawthorne lived for a while at the Farm," said Charlotte rather sharply. "How nice for him that he could choose whether or not to work. Some of us need to work so we can eat. And many of us at Brook Farm believe that the future of the country is lies with communities such as ours where everyone works and also has time to write poetry, or philosophy for that matter."

The young man soon wandered off to find more congenial company and Daniel turned to Charlotte with a smile. "You will never make a proper reporter." He shook his head in mock horror. "Perhaps we should keep our thoughts to ourselves and just ask questions."

"I'll try," Charlotte promised, "but I hope the others here aren't quite as pretentious as he is. Do you believe a poet has to be free of other work?"

"I certainly hope not or I fear my poetry will never see the light of day. But here comes our first speaker."

Daniel and Charlotte sat in the very last pew of the church where they could see the backs of the heads of almost everyone who was there. The heads were quite varied, most of them streaked with gray, some pure white, and a few glossy black or tawny blond. One heavyset patriarch had long, flowing pure white locks and massive shoulders that towered above everyone else in his pew.

The speaker was introduced as the Reverend Edgar Blackwell from Maine. He was a rather short, gray-haired man wearing a black clerical-style suit and large glasses. He opened a thick sheaf of notes and announced that he would talk about "Heathenish Attacks on Biblical Studies in the Modern Day". His theme seemed to be that Massachusetts was besieged by dangerous religious groups that did not respect the Christian traditions of the commonwealth. He talked for a long time and Charlotte's thoughts drifted off to the puzzle of Winslow Hopewell's death. They seemed to be learning nothing of any value here, but then she heard the Reverend Blackwell mention Quakers and her attention went back to him.

"Not only are ungodly freethinkers who deny the literal truth of the Bible dangerous, but also those who claim that every man can judge for himself the truth that God has given us. Those who call themselves Quakers refuse to accept the teaching of ordained ministers and believe God speaks to every human being and that each of us can choose his own truths. This can lead to schism and heresy. These people refuse to take oaths in a court of law. They refuse to remove their hats in our public buildings—even in churches." His voice sank to a low growl of disbelief as he said this.

"These Quakers do not believe in the sacredness of marriage. They allow a man and a woman to declare themselves married without the blessing of clergy. This undermines society and cannot be allowed. There is talk now of accepting Quaker marriages as equal to Christian weddings, but we must never allow that in Massachusetts."

After a while the Reverend Blackwell ran out of steam and his sermon petered out into a list of innovations that can never be allowed. Many in the audience stirred restlessly. At last he sat down and a very different speaker came to the pulpit. This was Bronson Alcott the tall white-haired man Charlotte had noticed earlier looking conspicuous in a pew near the front of the church. His manner was calm and quiet, but his words were lively, jumping about from one topic to another.

"Engage in nothing that cripples or degrades you. Your first duty is self-culture, self-exaltation: you may not violate this high trust. Either subordinate your vocation to your life or quit it forever. Your influence over others is commensurate with the strength that you have found in yourself."

Charlotte strained to understand what he meant. Could everyone do whatever they wanted? He went on and on talking about trusting your soul. He even mentioned Quakers and how they had taught him to believe the inner light that he found within himself. It was very different from Reverend Blackwell's view and Charlotte was glad that someone had a good word to say about Quakers, but she simply could not follow all of what he said. She looked at Daniel who was frowning deeply. He had brought paper with him to keep notes, but he wasn't writing much. Others seemed to be equally puzzled.

Finally other speakers became impatient and Alcott yielded his place. Speakers represented all shades of ideas. The man Daniel had seen at the April meeting was there insisting that the world would end in 1843 and there was no use trying to reform it. Another told the audience that cruelty to animals was the cause of evil and the world needed to be purified by everyone adopting a diet limited to grains and vegetables.

The Reverend John Carter, Fanny's friend and the minister of the church, spoke at last and he was brief and to the point. "While we are thinking of the many paths open to us in finding spiritual grace and build a better world, we should remember there are things we can do right now in Massachusetts to help destroy a great evil."

The change in tone was startling and the audience listened intently. Daniel started to write something on his papers.

"Slavery still exists in America," Reverend Carter continued, "And it is spreading across the country because of the pressure from representatives of the Southern states in Congress. The law requires anyone, in any state across the nation, to return runaway African slaves to their owners no matter how cruelly they have been treated. Many of us believe that obeying such a law is contrary to the law of God. The number of runaways increases day by day. Here at the church we have seen individuals, married couples, sometimes entire families fleeing their masters and seeking help in traveling to freedom in Canada. Let us not forget our duty to these poor fugitives among us."

John Carter was speaking very seriously but he did not mention any specifics of how to help runaways. Perhaps he was afraid there were Southern spies in the group. He was also the person responsible for organizing the Convention, at least so far as anyone could organize these eccentric people, so he moved on to practical matters. He suggested an adjournment to allow people a rest period. Many in the audience had brought food of some kind with them and the women of the parish had set up tables in the small parish hall and offered baked goods. Mrs. Carter was setting out platters of brown bread and biscuits and pitchers of milk. Fanny offered to help her and Charlotte joined the two of them in slicing bread and making sure that everyone got some.

Mrs. Carter was a brisk, small woman with gray hair and worried eyes. She fluttered her hands as she surveyed the large crowd, most of them large men who looked as though they expected far more food than was available.

"Do you think there is enough food?" Mrs. Carter fretted to Fanny, who murmured sympathetically, "Don't worry, Sarah, these men live should be able to live on their grand words; they scarcely need what we have to offer."

"Everyone was supposed to bring something, but these reformers never remember the worldly goods in life," Mrs. Carter looked as though she had seen enough reformers to last her a long time. The others smiled to think about how most of the men found their ideas far more important than their wives' baking and cooking, but the still wanted to eat when they were tired of talking. Charlotte realized that Mrs. Carter must have met many ministers who worked with her husband's church. Perhaps she had known Winslow Hopewell and would be willing to talk about him.

Daniel was talking to Bronson Alcott and another man. Actually he wasn't talking—he was listening. Very few people ever got a chance to talk when Mr. Alcott was part of the group. Charlotte was pleased to sit with Fanny and Mrs. Carter who were companionably exchanging recipes for baked beans. Finally she had a chance to ask Sarah Carter more about the runaways her husband had mentioned.

"Do you see these runaways very often? How do they get this far north?"

"Usually they stowaway on a ship to Boston and from there they follow a route, mostly up rivers, to Montreal in Lower Canada," Sarah Carter explained. "They stop at various farmhouses along the way where people are prepared to help them. Right now we are expecting a young couple from Virginia, although with winter coming on this is not a good time to travel."

"We had better not talk too much about this," cautioned Fanny. "Who knows who may be listening even in this room?"

Charlotte felt uncomfortable about restraining their talk, but she knew Fanny was probably right. There was another topic even more urgent, "Did you know Winslow Hopewell, Mrs. Carter? He died tragically at Brook Farm recently."

"Oh my yes, everyone has heard about that. What a terrible shock to the entire community! Poor old Reverend Thomas Hopewell will never get over the loss I'm afraid. And it is a blow to the entire church society. Ministers should not be involved in such scandalous crimes." Mrs. Carter's forehead was wrinkled with worry and sadness.

"It wasn't his fault," Charlotte said. "It's not a scandal when an innocent man is struck down."

"That depends on the cause," whispered Mrs. Carter darkly.

"What do you mean?" Fanny leaned across the table and whispered her question.

"My husband told me he had heard there were those who were deeply angry at young Reverend Hopewell. He was such a handsome young man that a few of the women in his congregation admired him all too well. I'll mention no names, but several men insisted their wives stop going to that church. One man even demanded that the whole family start attending church in a different parish."

"Did Winslow Hopewell ever act with impropriety?" Charlotte asked, scarcely able to believe what she was hearing. Would George Ripley have been friendly with a man of such bad reputation? Fanny sat still, one hand covering her mouth as she stared at Mrs. Carter.

They were sitting like that when the Reverend Carter stood up, clapped his hands, and said it was time to move back into the church for the rest of the program. Mrs. Carter jumped to her feet to clear away the dishes and Fanny and Charlotte slowly gathered their wits together and helped her. They had heard far more than they expected at this meeting, but Charlotte desperately needed to know more.

CHAPTER EIGHTEEN

Daniel Tries to Learn More

October 30, 1842.

Mealtime at the New Thinkers Convention was not a great success for Daniel. He was seated across the table from Bronson Alcott who talked on and on chasing an idea down byways and through brambles like a sheepdog herding a runaway flock. Just when he had said something worth hearing, he was off on something else, from the Great Oversoul to the necessity of every man becoming a God. He paid no attention to questions. The other men at the table didn't even try to get a word in and after a while Daniel stopped trying too.

Charlotte and Fanny chatted with Mrs. Carter. The three of them had their heads together all during the meal. As everyone walked back into the church for the afternoon session, Charlotte whispered to Daniel urgently, "I've learned something about Reverend Hopewell that may help us."

The talks during the afternoon ranged widely. New Thinkers had a lot to think about—everything from refusing to obey fugitive slave laws to the virtues of phrenology. That was a science, so the speaker claimed, that would let a practitioner discover a person's innermost talents and virtues by examining the contours of his skull. Daniel couldn't go along with the importance of bumps on the head. He'd seen people with all sizes and shapes of heads act pretty much the same.

When the meeting finally broke up, the sun was sinking fast and the sky was dark with snow clouds. Charlotte just had time to ask Daniel to meet her the following day so she could tell him what she had learned. Daniel walked back to Boston with a group of men who talked mostly about politics and not much about the ideas of the Convention. It was a relief to hear men worrying about money rather than about their souls.

Sunday morning was warmer with only a dusting of snow on the ground and not a cloud in the sky. Ruts in the road were frozen stiff so Daniel's boots didn't get too muddy except when he made a mistake and crashed through an ice-covered puddle. He passed a few wagonloads of folks headed for the churches in Boston, but no one was going his way.

Charlotte was waiting in the parlor and he was glad to sit down in front of the fire to warm up while they talked. She had a lacy kerchief around her neck and her cheeks were especially rosy. She was almost as pretty as Abigail, Daniel thought, as she leaned forward to talk.

"Mrs. Carter, the minister's wife, told us yesterday that some of the husbands of women in Reverend Hopewell's congregation were angry. They thought their wives were unsuitably attracted to him. One man in particular told his wife stop going to her minister for counsel and insisted that the whole family go to a different church."

"Whew!" Daniel whistled softly. "Did she mean that Hopewell was carrying on with women? That's a secret he would want to hide."

"She didn't say whether she thought he had misbehaved or whether the men were just suspicious. Either way it could have led to a quarrel and maybe even the crime."

"But who was that man? That's what we need to know."

"Mrs. Carter didn't mention any names and I don't know how we can find out without asking embarrassing questions," Charlotte admitted. "I did learn that the assistant minister at Reverend Hopewell's church has taken over the preaching. Could we ask him? Fanny said his name is Edgar Barlow."

The idea of going to the assistant minister was appealing but would it work? Maybe the man would be happy to talk scandal, but more likely he'd stick to his colleagues and deny that a minister would do anything wrong. He would rebuff any reporter who asked questions.

Charlotte had another idea and said, "Perhaps I could attend services at the church. People in the congregation are surely talking about the death of their minister. Some of the women might be indiscreet enough to say something to me. Perhaps they have vesper services this afternoon."

No sooner had she conceived the idea than she acted on it, running off to ask Mrs. Ripley whether she had any idea of church services at the Third Street Church. Daniel sat awkwardly in the parlor waiting for her return and trying to figure out a way to ask questions without seeming to. Fred interrupted him by entering, evidently from outside because his face was red from the cold and his knitted cap showed traces of snow. "You're here again?" he asked. "Is the

Farm so attractive, or is it just Miss Edgerton?" Before Daniel had to answer, Charlotte was back.

"The Third Street Church does indeed have afternoon vesper services and Mrs. Ripley said that it might be a nice tribute to Reverend Hopewell if some of us take the carriage and go into town to attend them. She said she would go with us."

Daniel's ears pricked up at the thought there might be a chance to ride into town like a gentleman instead of having another long walk. The charms of the frozen road, which had probably turned muddy in the sunshine by this time, were dwindling fast.

Fred spoke up, "Why don't we ride into the city together?"

They left for Boston early and were there in plenty of time for the afternoon service at the Third Street Church. Everyone piled out of the carriage and Mr. Gerritson drove it away to the public barn where the horses could keep warm until the service was over. Ellen and Daniel took the opportunity to visit their aunt while the others were at church.

Aunt Bridget looked exactly as she had the last time they had visited her. She was sitting at the same table sewing what seemed like the same bonnets, while two small children played on the floor around her. Ellen had brought some buns from dinner and she made tea because Aunt Bridget didn't want to stop her stitching. She said she had to have the black velvet bonnet ready on Monday morning.

Ellen passed on a little news from her mother, while Daniel watched the children finish their buns and start playing with the scraps of fabric. He reached into his pocket and pulled out a bit of string he'd been carrying around. They were delighted to have a new toy, and reminded Daniel of children in Ireland playing with any odds and ends they could get their hands on. No special toys for them. The O'Reilly's had come to America to get more for their children, but it didn't seem to amount to much.

At last the news session was over and Aunt Bridget turned to Daniel to ask how he was doing. "I'm not so bad," he said, "but I've been trying to investigate a death out at Brook Farm and it is very hard work. If I could solve this mystery, I think I could land a good newspaper job."

His aunt murmured sympathetically and wished him luck. She had heard of Winslow Hopewell. "He was that grand minister from the Third Street Church, wasn't he?" she asked. "Several of the women from that church buy my bonnets and I often hear them talking to one another about him."

"Did they talk about him indeed? I suppose they all admired him a great deal."

"Oh, it was more than admiring they were doing," she retorted. "The way they talked about his fashionable jackets and cravats they sounded more like schoolgirls than like married women talking about their minister. It wasn't his sermons they ever mentioned."

Ellen laughed. "Wouldn't you think they'd have more sense? Do you think they were flirting with their minister?"

"It's been heard of," Daniel answered. "These women don't have much on their minds with the servants taking care of their children and their husbands off at work all the time."

He turned to Aunt Bridget, "Do you remember any of the names of these women? Was there one particular woman who talked most about the minister?"

"Oh, indeed I know the names of all my clients. Many a woman buys a bonnet from me every year, sometimes one for the summer and one for winter. This black velvet one I'm working on now is for

Mrs. Jarrod Smith. I have to finish it for her by tomorrow so she can wear it to an important funeral."

"Is she one of the ones who talked about Winslow Homer?" Daniel asked hopefully.

She laughed, "Indeed no. Mrs. Smith is quite elderly and stern. I doubt she would ever have a frivolous thought about anyone, especially a minister. Now Mrs. Whitelaw, who wants the blue bonnet I'll be making tomorrow, she's a different kettle of fish entirely."

"What is she like?"

"She's young and flighty. Always changing her mind about what she wants. Should it be the blue or the green, and with the black fringe or the white feathers? She usually brings a friend or two with her when she comes and is always asking their opinion. She even asks my opinion. And then sometimes after she's gone home she'll send her maid around to tell me she's changed her mind again. She talks about the young minister all right. I've heard her say she wanted the white feathers on her bonnet so he'd be sure to look at her while he was preaching."

Daniel's spirits jumped when he heard that. A man whose wife picked out her bonnets to attract her minister could easily become jealous.

CHAPTER NINETEEN

Charlotte Plays a Part

October 30, 1842.

Many of the congregation smiled at Mrs. Ripley as she led the way to a pew near the front of the bare church. Soon a tall, thin man with coal black hair, blue eyes and unhealthily white skin mounted the tall pulpit. So this was Reverend Barlow. He was younger than Charlotte had expected and his voice was thin and reedy when he preached his short sermon about the dangers of celebrating the heathenish holiday of Halloween. Charlotte sighed listening to him, remembering guiltily that she was planning to help her pupils make a jack-o-lantern the next day.

Reverend Barlow paused to cough several times during his sermon, but he finally finished and it was time for the congregation to sing "Rock of Ages". An earnest man with a pitch pipe set the note and the congregation sang loudly. Charlotte heard Fanny's voice rise strong and clear just as it did when she sang with the children at the school.

When the service had ended, people moved slowly down the aisles toward the back of the church and lingered talking to one another. Charlotte looked closely at all of the women in the group, picking out the ones who wore bright and fashionable clothes. There were quite a few of them, but no one who stood out. Mrs. Ripley and Fanny had stopped to talk to a middle-aged friendly-looking couple and Charlotte joined them.

"Is your great enterprise out at Brook Farm thriving?" asked the man.

"It is doing as well as can be expected," Sophia Ripley answered gravely. "The members are working together to build up the farm and develop the school. It is difficult and wearying work."

"We need more members," Fanny burst in. "People like your-selves could benefit from sharing in the great dream of our Commu-nity. Have you ever thought of joining us?"

The man shifted slightly away from her as he replied thoughtful-ly, "My wife is not strong and we do not believe we could endure the rigors of setting up a new community."

Fanny's face grew quite red, "But how will society ever improve if those of us who have the means do not support important social efforts? Mr. Ripley and his wife are heroic in their effort to better the world. I do hope you will at least consider joining the enter-prise."

Sophia Ripley tried to stem the tide of words. "Now, Fanny, not everyone can be a member of our Community. We must understand that. Important though it is, we can work slowly and gradually build. As time goes by, my husband has perfect faith that many will join. And other, similar communities will spring up all across Massachu-setts, perhaps even further afield."

Her quiet voice soothed the couple. Finally the wife spoke up. "Yes, the Reverend Hopewell told us often about the great hope for the future that Brook Farm represents. He was optimistic that more and more people would come together to form new clusters of hope as he called them, but not all of us can be active participants."

Fanny was not mollified. Her face grew even more splotchy and red as she muttered, "But the Reverend Hopewell was not prepared to work with us. He made promises that were not fulfilled."

Mrs. Ripley spoke up quickly. "His life has been cut tragically short. We cannot blame him for things left undone when he died." The couple nodded in agreement and turned away.

As the three women left the church to meet Mr. Gerritson for the trip back to the Farm, Ellen and Daniel joined them. Daniel whispered to Charlotte, "I will write to you tonight. I have learned a lot and I have a task you might be able to undertake on Wednesday."

On Monday evening teachers and students at Brook Farm gathered for a small Halloween celebration. Charlotte watched the children laugh as they went bobbing for apples in Mrs. Geary's big laundry tub. Timothy Pretlove was the boldest of boys and chased the largest apple around with determination until he finally caught it in his teeth; but, by this time, his clothes were soaked and Abigail had to fetch him dry ones. Catching the apple on a string kept everyone dry but the children became almost hysterical with hilarity as they watched one another chase the errant apple in circles. Despite the noise Charlotte was glad to see them so cheerful. It had been a somber few weeks and even the youngest child felt some of the strain.

On Tuesday, Daniel's note arrived in the mail:

Dear Miss Edgerton,

My aunt, Bridget O'Reilly told me that several members of the Third Street Church bought bonnets from her. You remember that she is a

seamstress and a skilled one too. In describing some of the women, she men-
tioned one whose behavior made me think she might have aroused her hus-
band's jealousy. This woman, Mrs. Whitelaw, is expecting to receive her
latest bonnet on Wednesday afternoon. I have arranged with Mrs. O'Reilly
to pick up the bonnet from her so that you can make the delivery. It seems
to me that a clever girl like yourself might be able to learn a great deal
from Mrs. Whitelaw in the course of delivering the bonnet. Are you willing
to try?

I will come to meet you at Brook Farm at dinnertime on
Wednesday and bring the bonnet. If you agree, we can walk to Mrs. White-
law's house together and you can make the delivery.

Your respectful friend,

Daniel Gallagher

Charlotte wasn't sure what she thought about the scheme. How
could she ask questions about Reverent Hopewell without arousing
the woman's suspicions? But maybe this would be the key to the
whole thing. She was nervous, but willing to try.

Finally Wednesday came and Daniel arrived before dinner was
over. Charlotte saw him walking to the kitchen door carrying a
leather hatbox. The day was bright and Charlotte looked forward to
a brisk trip. As they walked she had a chance to ask questions. "What
have you been up to since I saw you? You don't spend all your time
wondering about Reverend Hopewell's death, do you?"

"Oh no, I have to earn enough to pay my room and board to Mrs.
Costello. This week I've been sitting in the Court House and writing
up cases of thievery and cheating for the *Transcript.* I could make a
better living doing that if Boston weren't so law-abiding. It's dull
listening to people squabbling over whether the right weight of po-

tatoes was delivered to a grocer or whether the surveyor cheated on the boundary of the lot for a mansion."

"Still, it's not a bad way to make a living at least compared to working hard on a farm like my father had to do. It wore him down a lot more than sitting in a courtroom like a gentleman."

"I won't argue with you. That's one reason I want to be a newspaperman. When the court is not in session I have to go down to the docks and find work unloading ships in the harbor. I'd a lot sooner wear a suit when I work."

They walked along companionably and soon were at the outskirts of Boston. Daniel knew the way to Mrs. Whitelaw's house, which was set on one of the most elegant streets in the city. They walked to the back door and found themselves facing a white-haired woman in a black dress.

"I've come to deliver Mrs. Whitelaw's bonnet," Charlotte said. "Mrs. O'Reilly said she wanted to have it today."

"Yes indeed, it's time you got here." said the woman, who must have been the housekeeper. "Molly will show you upstairs to Mrs. Whitelaw's sitting room. You can stay in the kitchen, young man," she added sternly to Daniel.

Molly led Charlotte into a broad hallway that faced the front door of the mansion. The deep-piled maroon carpeting felt soft as a cloud and Charlotte admired herself in the gold-rimmed mirror they passed. Molly knocked on one of the doors and then opened it letting a flood of light into the hall.

The room had blue and white paper on the walls and the furniture was white with blue upholstery. On a small sofa across from the door, a woman in a blue dress was reading a book. She looked up and saw Charlotte carrying the hatbox and said to the maid, "Thank you, Bridget. You may go back to the kitchen now."

Charlotte winced when she heard her call poor Molly "Bridget" but most people called all their Irish servants either Bridget or Paddy as if it was too much trouble to learn their names. Still, Mrs. Whitelaw had a pleasant face and she smiled as Charlotte opened the box and brought out the blue velvet bonnet.

"Let me try it on," she cried happily, taking it and setting it on her blonde hair. Twisting and turning in front of the white-framed mirror she admired her image. "What do you think?" she asked Charlotte. "Should the bow be larger?"

Charlotte was at a loss. She had no idea how a fashionable bonnet should look. Mrs. Whitelaw impulsively placed the hat on Charlotte's head and tied the bows. "Now let me see how it looks on someone else. Oh, tilt your head a little flirtatiously. You stand like a block of wood. I wish my sister were here to help me."

Charlotte smiled and twisted her head around, trying to feel like a lady. She glanced in the mirror. The bonnet made her look quite fetching, but she quickly shook her head at those idle thoughts and turned to her task.

"This is a beautiful bonnet, Mrs. Whitelaw. I'm sure Mr. Whitelaw will admire you in it."

"Oh, husbands never notice what their wives wear! Mr. Whitelaw has his nose buried in his account books all day long—most evenings too. He'll never even know I have a new bonnet."

"I am sure that many people will admire your bonnet, Mrs. Whitelaw."

"My friends will admire it no doubt, and be jealous that it looks so well on me. I will certainly wear it to church next Sunday..." she broke off and sighed deeply. "But even at church there is no one to truly see me anymore. Since dear Reverend Hopewell is gone there is no one. Poor Reverend Barlow is a callow youth scarcely out of the schoolroom. I cannot bear it that Reverend Hopewell is dead."

Mrs. Whitelaw pulled a handkerchief out and began sobbing into it. Charlotte stood dumbly waiting for her to recover herself. Instead the woman threw herself down on the sofa again and sobbed more loudly, waving her hand toward the door. "Leave! Leave! You can tell Mrs. O'Reilly I will send her money in a day or two. And tell Bridget to bring me a cup of tea. I am not at all well."

After that firm dismissal, Charlotte turned and went downstairs to the kitchen. She told the cook that Mrs. Whitelaw wanted tea and then she and Daniel left. Out on the street again the darkness was coming quickly. Charlotte didn't fancy the long walk back to Brook Farm, but there was no choice. Daniel, however, was playing the gentleman. He informed her that he had arranged to borrow his landlady's wagon so he could drive her safely home.

"I'll not have you wandering along the road at night," he insisted. "Not after what happened to Reverend Hopewell. And after all, you can't trust those Irish ruffians on the roads these days." Charlotte laughed and told him he was quite enough of a ruffian.

As they rode back to the Farm she told him about Mrs. Whitelaw and her grief at the loss of Winslow Hopewell.

"Those tears are enough to tell us that her husband might be jealous," said Daniel. "We must find him and ask a few questions. As the owner of such a mansion he must be well known in the city. I asked the cook a few questions and found out he owns several whaling vessels. I'll go down to the docks tomorrow and find where he spends his time. We may be solving this mystery at last."

CHAPTER TWENTY

Daniel Searches the Docks

November 3, 1842.

Daniel woke to a gray and threatening morning, but he felt rested and happy. His talk with Charlotte the day before made him think they were finally moving ahead on finding answers. Charlotte understood how important solving the crime would be to his future. She was becoming as close a friend as the ones he had back in Galway; for the first time since coming to Boston he had an American friend. It wasn't someone who shared his heritage but someone who shared his hopes and ambitions.

As he pulled on his work clothes, Daniel decided he'd nose around the docks seeing what he could find out about Mr. Whitelaw. If he owned whaling ships, he would surely have an office somewhere in the dock area. Daniel could locate the office and maybe talk to a couple of the officers on his ships. He could pretend to be looking for a berth, not too convincingly though or he might find himself shanghaied and off on some long voyage.

As he got near the docks the smell of fish hung over everything. The street alongside the water was dirty with muddy footprints and half-gnawed dead fish that had been worked over by the dogs. A torn, discarded newspaper blew listlessly across the brick pavement. Daniel could recognize the whaling ships by their equipment—the brick furnace on deck and the whaleboats hanging over the sides. He stopped alongside of one called *Lark* to talk to a wizened old sailor sitting on a barrel mending a rope.

"Have you been out on the *Lark*?" Daniel asked. "Is she a good ship? I need to earn a packet of money so as to pay off some debts."

"She's made a lot of money on this last trip," the seaman spit into the water. "Whales were running off Patagonia and the price of oil is high right now."

"How's the captain?"

"A fair man. He won't stand for no nonsense and no laziness, but he divvies up the food and drink fair enough and shares out the pay at the end with no holding back and no favorites."

"Sometimes it's the owners who are greedy and shortchange everyone. Do you know who owns this rig?"

"A fellow called Whitelaw. I never saw him but once—a frosty-faced skinny guy, but no complaints from the men."

Daniel was relieved that Mr. Whitelaw owned this ship. At least he hadn't wasted time asking questions for nothing. Now to track the man down and take a look at him in person. The sailor was finishing his mending and heading off, but he turned to Daniel.

"That's a lot of news I gave you young man," he said. "Makes a man thirsty talking so much."

Daniel took the hint and walked him to the nearest tavern for a pint of ale. He soon learned that Whitelaw's office—"Whitelaw and Brown" it was called—was a walk up Beacon Street from the dock. That was his next stop as soon as he could figure out how to find out what Whitelaw had been up to during the past few weeks.

Whitelaw's office was in a small, dark building with a chandler's shop on the ground floor. Through the small, dim window, Daniel could see coils of rope and a shelf full of tools. He walked upstairs, knocked at the door and heard a gruff, "Come In" and was soon facing a thin, tall man in a black suit seated at a large desk. A ledger was open in front of him and at the side of the office were two small standing desks where clerks were copying figures into other ledgers. Two small windows let in some light, but it was dim and the clerks bent over their books straining to see the figures.

"What do you want?" asked the man at the desk. "I'm a busy man so don't waste my time trying to sell me something. I don't need any officers on my ships at this time and if you're a seaman you'd better go down to the dock to find out about work. Don't waste my time."

"I am not looking for a position," Daniel answered trying to sound like a proper Bostonian. "I am a newspaperman and I am writing a tribute to the Reverend Winslow Hopewell, who died tragically only a few weeks ago. I understand you were a leading member of his congregation at the Third Street Church, so I would like to ask you a few questions that would help me. I would like the kind of personal details about the Reverend Hopewell's faith and charity that endeared him to the congregation and made his loss so painful to the entire city."

Mr. Whitelaw did not respond with the gracious reply Daniel had hoped for. Instead he scowled as though he'd been given something bitter to chew on. "What business is it of yours what Reverend Hopewell was like or about his private hope? Let churchmen write about one another and praise each other to the skies. I have no time for airy speeches about churchly virtues."

"The people of the city will feel the loss of the Reverend Hopewell. It would comfort them to be able to read about his life and work. It is edifying to dwell on the virtues of the clergy and I believe Winslow Hopewell had a large following. I have heard that many of the women in his congregation were overcome with grief when they heard of his passing."

Mr. Whitelaw screwed his lips up in distaste as if he had bitten into a walnut and found a worm. "Just because silly women wail and carry on, that doesn't mean the man was composed of all virtue. To give Reverend Hopewell his due, he preached a sensible sermon and often extolled the importance of faithfulness in marriage and honesty in business. But he was well-known while he was alive and needs no further memorializing in his death, certainly not in any public newspaper."

"Perhaps you could recommend to me someone who might be willing to talk just a little about the Reverend. Perhaps one of the women of the congregation could help our readers understand why he appealed so much to the female mind. Many young ministers could learn a great deal from his example. Could I perhaps speak to your wife and ask her a few questions about him?"

"Get out of my office, young man. I forbid you to speak to my wife for any reason whatsoever! Your questions would only increase her grief and your presence would sully our home. I want to hear no more of newspaper stories."

With that he walked over to the door and jerked it open. The two clerks were eying the scene surreptitiously from beneath their eyeshades. Daniel ran quickly down the stairs and out the door. Mr. Whitelaw had certainly made himself a suspect with his harsh reaction to questions.

The first thing Daniel had to do was go to the newspaper office to find more information about Mr. Whitelaw. He was a wealthy ship owner, so there must have been some news stories about him and his business. Was he on any of the civic committees in the city or was he an important political figure?

When Daniel went to the *Transcript* office, he brought Mr. Cabot the stories he had written about cases that had come before the magistrate during the week. There weren't any spectacular crimes or misdeeds, but Mr. Cabot was pleased.

"These will fill a good column for tomorrow's paper," he said. "You have a clear hand, Daniel. I've half a mind to make you one of my clerks."

"Thanks you, sir, but I'd rather try to be a newspaperman. I am still trying to solve the mystery of who killed Reverend Hopewell and I think I have a good notion who it might be. I'd like to read some of the back numbers of the paper to see whether I can find more."

Mr. Cabot raised his bushy eyebrows and looked at Daniel over the top of his glasses. "I think you're chasing moonshine, young man. The sooner you settle down to a good steady clerk's job the better off you'll be, but you can look at as many newspapers as you want in the back room."

The walls of the back room were lined with shelves holding stacks of newspapers neatly arranged according to the year and month. Where was he to start? Daniel figured he might as well work backward from yesterday's paper. It was slow, tedious work. The inky pages soon turned his fingers black and the smell of them tickled his nose. The room was very quiet. He heard Mr. Cabot go out, telling the clerks he would return after dinner. After that there was no sound except the scratch of the clerks' pens and the rustle of pages turning.

After searching for an hour, Daniel was beginning to think Mr. Whitelaw must be the quietest and most law-abiding man in the Commonwealth. Then he finally found a mention of him. He was listed as one of the sponsors of the Annual Fourth of July celebration where he introduced the main speaker, Daniel Webster. That was no use so he kept searching. Next he found a mention of Whitelaw as the "well-known owner of the whaling ships *Lark* and *Eagle*" which had arrived in harbor with the largest cargo of whale oil and ivory ever landed in Boston. It was no wonder he was so wealthy. But what kind of man was he? Had he ever been involved in anything disreputable? Was he a man who could kill his pastor out of jealousy?

Finally Daniel found an odd note in an unexpected place. He had been searching primarily the shipping news and civic reports, but in one paper he glanced at the column of Lectures and Exhibits and the name Whitelaw leapt out. It was not Mr. Whitelaw, nor his wife, but a Miss Tabitha Whitelaw who was mentioned as a leading member of the Massachusetts Anti-Slavery Society. The Society had sponsored a luncheon talk by Miss Margaret Fuller at Miss Whitelaw's home. The date on the newspaper was November 10, 1840, almost exactly two years ago.

All of the threads in Boston seemed to connect. If Margaret Fuller was a friend of Tabitha Whitelaw, perhaps Charlotte could find out from her more about Mr. Benjamin Whitelaw and what sort of man he was. Not that his sister would say a bad word about him, but she might let slip something about his temper. Daniel decided to write to Charlotte and suggest that she might call on Miss Fuller.

First though he would make another effort to find out more about the habits of the man. It was about the time of day when he would leave his office. You can tell a great deal about a man by whether he goes straight home to his wife and family or whether he lingers at a tavern or pays a call on a friend. Daniel hurried down to the dockside again where the fog rolling in made the streets darker than they were uptown. There was still a light in the window of Whitelaw's office, so he stationed himself across the street to watch.

In just a few minutes the light went out upstairs and someone appeared at the door carrying a small lantern. He paused for a minute to look around and started walking briskly up Beacon St. toward a more pleasant neighborhood. Daniel could tell by his height that it must be Mr. Whitelaw so he followed him as inconspicuously as possible. Not that there was any need to worry. Several clumps of sailors were strolling up the street talking loudly and now and then singing a snatch of song. They would have drowned out footsteps even if he'd worn hobnailed boots. Mr. Whitelaw paid no attention to the sailors or anything else, but walked swiftly to the corner of West Street where he turned abruptly to the right.

Daniel had just turned the corner when he saw Whitelaw walk up the steps to one of the small gray houses on the street. It was a neat enough little cottage and well-kept, but nothing like the mansion where Whitelaw lived. When Whitelaw knocked, the door was opened by a little servant girl; behind her Daniel glimpsed a tall woman in a gray dress who held out her hands to greet Whitelaw. He entered and the door closed quickly behind him.

What did this mean? Did Mr. Whitelaw have his own flirtations to carry on? Surely he should have been going straight home to his wife if he was an honest man. Daniel wondered what went on in that mansion of the Whitelaws. He would certainly have plenty of news to give Charlotte in his letter.

CHAPTER TWENTY ONE

Charlotte Pays a Call

November 4, 1842

On Friday morning as Charlotte's young students struggled to copy the words she had written on the large slate at the front of the class, Charlotte couldn't get her mind off Mrs. Whitelaw. Why would a woman who led such a comfortable life become entangled with her minister? Most women were struggling to feed their children and take care of their husbands while Violet Whitelaw wasted her time fussing about bonnets. Did she ever have a serious thought in her head? She wouldn't lift a finger to make the world better. Thinking about all the women like her made Charlotte gloomy, so she dismissed her class a little early for dinner and went downstairs where she discovered a note from Daniel:

Dear Miss Edgerton,

Yesterday I learned much of interest. I visited Mr. Benjamin Whitelaw in his office and inquired about Reverend Hopewell. My reception was unfriendly and when I asked permission to speak to Mrs. Whitelaw, I was ordered to leave the premises. There is undoubtedly bad feeling there about Reverend Hopewell.

Perhaps the most interesting news I was able to learn from newspaper files is that Mr. Whitelaw has a sister named Tabitha Whitelaw who appears to be acquainted with Margaret Fuller. Do you think it might be possible for you to inquire from Miss Fuller about the Whitelaws? Is she still visiting your Community? She might be able to tell us more about Mr. Whitelaw's habits and his nature. Another oddity I discovered about the man is that when he left his office last night he did not go immediately to his home, but to another house where he appeared to be visiting a lady. I am growing very curious about Mr. Whitelaw's habits.

May I call on you this coming Sunday so we can talk further about what we have discovered?

Your respectful friend,

Daniel Gallagher

Daniel's news strengthened Charlotte's belief that Mr. Whitelaw had a grudge against Winslow. She found it hard to believe that such a respectable man would commit murder, but a quarrel can easily lead to unplanned violence. She had seen men in taverns beat a man half to death in a fight over a missing calf or a spilled pint of ale.

Miss Fuller was staying with friends at nearby Spring Hill, so Charlotte made plans to pay a visit. On Saturday afternoon after dinner she set out with Ellen, a great admirer of Miss Fuller, who was glad to have a chance to see her heroine. They trudged along the heavily rutted dirt road past brown fields covered with a skim of snow. A pair of clumsy young collies barked at them from an isolated farmhouse, but not a soul was visible around the house or barn. Winter was closing in.

At Spring Hill, they quickly identified the house where Miss Fuller was staying. It was the largest house in the tiny village and the only one that looked as though it would have room for entertaining visitors. Charlotte knocked boldly at the front door and they were soon inside a warm, friendly-looking hallway. Miss Fuller seemed pleased to see them; she was the only one at home except for the cook and housekeeper because her hosts had driven into Boston to buy supplies for the coming cold weather.

The front parlor was austerely furnished with dark upholstered chairs, a large bookcase and a small desk. Charlotte enjoyed sitting in front of the fire blazing in the brick fireplace. After a few polite exchanges, she launched into her questions.

"We are trying to discover the person responsible for the Reverend Hopewell's death," she began. "The sheriff has decided that it was a misadventure caused by an unknown person and he is no longer interested in searching for the culprit. I am determined to continue searching and so is our friend Daniel Gallagher, who works for the *Transcript.*"

"I applaud your determination," said Miss Fuller, "but I don't believe I can help you find any answers."

"Oh, but wait until you hear what we have discovered," Ellen broke in eagerly.

"Our friend Mr. Gallagher," Charlotte continued "has discovered that some of the men in the congregation of the Third Street Church were rather angry at Reverend Hopewell." She felt herself blushing as she said that and a slight smile crossed Miss Fuller's face.

"Do you think they were jealous of Reverend Hopewell's influence over their wives?" she asked.

"Yes, it has been known to happen that clergymen are indiscreet. In particular we are curious about Mr. and Mrs. Whitelaw. I have spoken with Mrs. Whitelaw and she appears to be overcome with grief caused by Reverend Hopewell's death while her husband became very angry at Mr. Gallagher when asked questions about the man. He seems to harbor anger at the minister. I believe you might know the Whitelaws and perhaps Miss Tabitha Whitelaw too."

Miss Fuller was silent for a few minutes and appeared to be deep in thought. Finally she spoke. "I know Tabitha Whitelaw quite well. She attended several of my Conversations a few years ago and I have met her at various gatherings. She is a very serious person and devoted to causes such as the abolition of slavery. It is mainly in connection with this work that I have seen her. I know her brother and sister-in-law much less well, but I have met them.

"Violet Whitelaw is considerably younger than her husband and his sister. She has two young children and appears to be very devoted to them. She is not from Boston, not even from New England, I believe, but from Virginia. Perhaps that is why she does not strongly support Tabitha's devotion to abolition. I have never seen them quarrel, but at a large reception once I noticed that Violet Whitelaw was fluttering about the room talking gaily to many of the men there and paying very little attention to Tabitha's efforts to engage the group in serious conversation. Benjamin Whitelaw seems to be quite proud of his wife's beauty and charm."

"Does he have a harsh temper?" Charlotte asked. "Do you think he might resort to violence if he thought his wife was doing something he deemed inappropriate?"

Miss Fuller was quiet for a long minute, while the cook came in with a tray bearing a teapot, three teacups and a plate of biscuits.

"Thank you, Mary," said Margaret Fuller with a smile in her voice. "It's very thoughtful of you to have brought us tea."

As she poured the tea and offered biscuits, she shook her head firmly as though she had come to a decision. "I believe I should tell you the story that Tabitha Whitelaw told me about her brother. It might have a bearing on the events here."

Ellen and Charlotte leaned forward with anticipation as she began to speak.

"Some fifteen years ago Benjamin Whitelaw was the first mate on a ship that brought molasses from the West Indies to Boston to be made into rum. The hold was full of cargo, such a large haul that many of the stores were lashed to the the masts on deck. About two days out of Kingston, he was walking the deck at sunrise one morning making sure that everything was in order when he heard a faint noise from behind one of the barrels. It sounded like someone singing. He immediately pulled the barrels and bales aside and discovered a skinny young African huddled behind the stores.

"When Whitelaw hauled him out and demanded to know his business, the youth replied he was fleeing from a cruel slave master who had often beaten him because he was not strong enough to work all day in the sugarcane fields. He was trying to make his way to Canada, which he had heard was the promised land of freedom.

"As a ship's officer Whitelaw knew his duty was to report the runaway to the Captain, but he also knew the Captain was a Southerner who had worked in the slave trade for many years before it was outlawed. A runaway slave could expect no mercy from him. Despite twinges of conscience, Whitelaw determined to hide the runaway and help him escape when the ship reached Boston.

"The days went by as the ship made slow progress north. Winds were not favorable and the crew grew unruly as the days grew longer and their hopes of making it home seemed fainter. And of course as the days passed, the store of supplies on deck dwindled and the runaway's hiding place grew less secure. Finally, late one evening when Whitelaw was in charge of the vessel, he heard a commotion on deck. He investigated and found that the ship's cook, a massive man, had discovered the runaway and hauled him out of his hiding place. He was pursuing the boy with a meat cleaver as the boy tried frantically to escape. Ordered to stop, the cook paid no heed but continued forcing the boy back toward the railing. Finally Whitelaw moved in to stop the cook, but as he moved toward the fighting pair, the cook gave the boy a final push and he fell to the deck hitting his head on a stanchion. It was apparent that he was dead.

"Whitelaw was so incensed at the ferocity of the cook's attack that he rushed at the man and started giving him a thrashing. By this time the noise of the fight attracted a circle of spectators who soon realized Whitelaw would likely kill the cook in his turn. They pulled him off before he could dispatch the cook. At last the captain appeared and gave orders that Whitelaw be confined to his quarters for the day. The runaway was unceremoniously dumped overboard and the cook, as Tabitha tells it, was punished by being deprived of his ration of rum for a week. After all, he had only injured a runaway who should not have been on the ship at all.

"There were no charges brought against Whitelaw, but when the ship returned to Boston the captain spread word about the incident. He claimed Whitelaw was a hothead who might cause trouble and warned other captains not to take him on. That was the end of Whitelaw's career as a ship's officer. It certainly proves that he has a quick, sharp temper, although he seems to have controlled it for these last fifteen years. He became a merchant, earned a lot of money, and has been a leading citizen of the city."

Ellen and Charlotte were enthralled by the story. What sort of man was this who showed such great kindness toward a helpless runaway, but such vicious cruelty to the man who bullied him? Was he the sort of man who might strike and kill an innocent clergyman because his wife found him too attractive?

"That's a heroic story," Ellen commented. "Do you think he would have killed the cook if he had not been stopped? Do you think he is capable of killing?"

Margaret Fuller leaned back in her chair and pulled her gray shawl closer around her shoulders as she said, "Vengeance is mine, saith the Lord. That's what the Bible tells us, isn't it? Yet I can't help honoring a man who tries to save a poor wretched runaway. I was of two minds about telling you this story. I am not sure a man should be a suspect because of the violence he showed when he was young."

Charlotte found herself sighing and shaking her head. "Nothing is easy, is it? What are the pieces we can put together? Benjamin Whitelaw seems to have been troubled by his wife's flirtation with Winslow Hopewell. He has a history of taking it upon himself to punish a man who is doing wrong. Is that what happened? He could have gone to Brook Farm to talk to Reverend Hopewell and ask him to refrain from having contact with his wife. Then perhaps he was seized by jealously and struck out angrily without thinking of the consequences. But how are we to know for sure?"

"Can you find out whether or not he went there?" asked Margaret Fuller. "Surely a man like Benjamin Whitelaw would have ridden a horse, or perhaps driven a buggy out to the Farm for an early morning visit. Did anyone see him? Is there any evidence of a horse being in the area?"

"The recent rain and snow would surely have destroyed any traces of an animal being there," Charlotte admitted slowly. "We will have to find a different way to discover what happened."

CHAPTER TWENTY TWO

Daniel Has a Disappointing Day

November 6, 1842.

Daniel had promised to visit Charlotte after dinner on Sunday and he was waiting for her when the Brook Farmers started clearing their tables. The smell of molasses and beans made his mouth water although he had eaten a rasher of bacon and an egg at the boarding house. In the parlor someone was playing the piano, lovely music with trills and flourishes that made him stop for a moment to listen. But he was impatient and eager to talk to Charlotte privately. He had no time to enjoy music today and suggested they take a walk.

November is not the best month for a walk in Massachusetts and the wind was harsh, blowing the crows backwards when they tried to fly into it, but the sun was bright. Charlotte told him the strange story about how Benjamin Whitelaw had protected a runaway African stowaway on his ship and then attacked the man who had struck him down and caused his death. That seemed to prove that Whitelaw was a hothead even though he was a respectable middle-aged Boston businessman. Daniel couldn't picture him either protecting an African or attacking another officer, but there's many a man who has committed rash acts in his youth.

"He might have attacked Winslow Hopewell if he was angry enough about the way the minister was attracting his wife. Don't you think so?" asked Charlotte.

"Yes, I suppose he might. But the sheriff won't be convinced of his guilt just because he was in a fight fifteen years ago. We need to know more than that."

"We have to find out whether he was anywhere near Brook Farm when Reverend Hopewell died. Did he have his horse or buggy out here that morning? If we could find out that he went out early that morning, we would be closer to the answer," suggested Charlotte.

"You're right. Tracking down the horse is the only way to find out. And that's up to me because I can't see you wandering around Boston stables looking for a horse."

"I could, if I had too," insisted Charlotte. "But it will be easier for you. All you have to do is look like an unemployed stable hand looking for a job." She eyed his clothes and then added mischievously, "That shouldn't be too hard for you."

Daniel huffed a bit thinking she had no right to criticize his clothes even though he wasn't wearing his best suit. He had to save that to impress Mr. Cabot. But Charlotte was laughing now and Daniel knew she meant no harm. She had been a poor girl herself and knew what it was like to be always worrying about saving good clothes for when they were really needed.

By the time they got back to the Hive, their cheeks were red and their hands numb with cold, but they sat by the fire in the kitchen for a while and soon felt better. Daniel was cheerful when he headed back to Boston late in the afternoon.

The next morning he was up early and set out for the Whitelaw mansion. It wasn't hard to find the stable behind the house, a smallish brick building with a turret. In the stable yard a gray-haired man in work clothes was saddling up a glossy chestnut horse. Daniel slouched over toward him trying to look like a down-and-out stable hand looking for an odd job.

"Have you any need of help?" he called out to the man.

"Not from the likes of you."

"I've experience working with horses," Daniel lied. "Lost my last place when the owner went bankrupt, but I'm a hard worker. This is Mr. Whitelaw's stable, is it?"

"Yes, it is and he's very particular who works for him. We don't need any help now."

"I've heard he's a good man to work for and not likely to go bankrupt anytime soon. How many horses does he have here? You must be worked off your feet in a big place like this." Daniel tried to sound sympathetic. The man's face was weather beaten and he had a scar across his cheek. He looked as though he'd been working hard for a long time.

"It's not too bad. Mr. Whitelaw's a fair enough man. And his wife has a ready smile and doesn't complain the way some Boston ladies do. But I've told you already, we don't need more help." His voice got louder as he said those last words.

"What's the trouble, Harry?" said a voice behind him. It was Mr. Whitelaw, one person Daniel didn't want to see. He pulled his cap down over his forehead and turned his head away as he moved toward the driveway.

"Just looking for a job. Guess I picked the wrong place," Daniel mumbled as he moved as fast as he could. He almost got past White-law too, but then he felt a hand seize his shoulder.

"Say, aren't you the young fella who works for the *Transcript?*" Mr. Whitelaw bellowed. "What are you doing hanging around my home? You'll pay for this. I'm taking you to the sheriff."

"I've done nothing wrong," Daniel protested. "What complaint would you make to the sheriff?"

"Trespassing, you fool!"

"I've a right to look for a job and I'm leaving your property right now." Daniel moved as quickly as he could.

Mr. Whitelaw was flushed with anger, but he must have realized the sheriff wouldn't arrest a man for asking about a job. He content-ed himself with shaking his riding crop after Daniel and spluttering, "I'll see you never work for John Cabot again."

Daniel realized he'd made a hash of that. What was the point of trying to solve the mystery if Mr. Cabot refused to print it? Maybe if he rushed over to Mr. Cabot's office and explained that he'd been working to solve the mystery, he could get away with it. But he couldn't go face him in his work clothes, he'd have to change at the boarding house and hope Whitelaw would have some urgent busi-ness to attend to before he talked to Cabot.

When Daniel got to the *Transcript* office, Mr. Cabot had not even arrived. He waited impatiently while the clerks kept scratching away with their pens. The room was very quiet. Finally there was a noise on the stairs and Mr. Cabot came in.

"Good morning, young man. Have you solved the great crime of the century out at Brook Farm yet?" He seemed in a friendly mood so Daniel breathed a sigh of relief.

"I've been continuing my investigations, sir," he began and at that moment heard a sharp rap at the door. Mr. Whitelaw walked in accompanied by the man with the gold watch chain Daniel had seen before in the office. Whitelaw burst out talking, not caring who he interrupted.

"This young man has been pursuing me. I've half a mind to charge him with trespass for coming to my stable this morning and bothering my stable man. It's a disgrace that he's working for a paper like the *Transcript*. He's no credit to you and I hope you will dismiss him at once."

"Sir, I was following an important lead in the story. I brought no harm to Mr. Whitelaw and caused no trouble. When I get the full story and the details are clear, you will see that I've damaged no one who is an upstanding member of the community."

Mr. Cabot's thin lips twisted with distaste as he listened to the two of them, but his scowl was directed at Daniel. "These two men are leading citizens of Boston and stockholders in the newspaper too. Mr. Whitelaw and Mr. Jarrod Smith are not to be bothered with your wild schemes."

At this point Mr. Smith spoke up. He had an oddly high, squeaky voice for such a substantial man. "Not that we don't want to read good stories in the *Transcript*," he said. "The people of our city like to read the latest news. And we mustn't let it all go to other newspapers."

Now Mr. Cabot was torn between pleasing Mr. Whitelaw by telling Daniel to get out and never show his face again and pleasing Mr. Smith by going for a big story that would increase newspaper sales. In the end he tried to have it both ways.

"You must leave Mr. Whitelaw alone and stay away from his house, Daniel. I've half a mind to order you out of this office but I'll give you one more chance. It you come up with the real story about how Reverend Hopewell died and who was responsible, you can bring it to me and I'll publish it."

"Yes sir, Mr. Cabot. I'm sure I can come up with the story soon," Daniel said and skedaddled out of there as fast as he could, leaving the three men to work out their own differences. The only problem was that he was no closer to knowing where Mr. Whitelaw had been on the day Hopewell died than he had been when he started out.

He walked slowly up the street trying to figure out how he could find out about Whitelaw's actions. He couldn't ask Mrs. Whitelaw. Her husband would find out for sure and they'd all come down on him like a cannonball. That would be the end of his newspaper career. Who else would know Whitelaw's habits? His clerks? They looked like timid white-faced mice who wouldn't open their mouths for fear of their boss. Then Daniel had an idea. What about the woman he had gone to see when he left the office the night Daniel followed him? Who was she? And how much would she know about what he was up to?

The sun was high in the sky now, so walking was comfortable. Daniel followed the route he had taken that night and was soon at the corner where Mr. Whitelaw had turned. Walking down on the opposite side of the street keeping his eyes open he found the right house easily enough. He remembered the neat white trim around the windows. No one was in sight and no sign of life came from the house. It might be hours before anyone went in or out.

Thinking hard he walked back to Beacon Street and found a small tavern where he could just see a corner of the house if he looked sharp. The place was not one he would have chosen to linger in, but there was not much choice. He ordered a plate of fishcakes and a pint of ale and sat close to the small, grimy window facing the street. After half an hour of idling, he saw a woman come out the door with a shopping basket over her arm. She looked like the maid he had seen the other night, so he left some coins for the tavern keeper and followed her.

The woman kept a brisk pace down the street until she came to the bakeshop and went inside. She was talking to the woman who kept the shop, standing at the counter where Daniel could see loaves of various sizes. He stepped up alongside her and studied the breads closely.

"Those loaves are a penny each," said the bakeshop keeper looking sharply at Daniel. "If you have the money, you can take one."

"I have money enough. I've trying to choose one that will tempt my mother. She's feeling poorly and not eating as well as we'd like. I've never had to shop for her before."

That softened both women and they began giving advice about tempting his mother's appetite with a spoonful of wine or honey. The maid spoke up, "My mistress, Miss Tabitha, always says a dose of honey in hot tea will restore anyone's appetite."

"Is that Miss Tabitha Whitelaw?" Daniel asked.

"Indeed it is. Do you know Miss Whitelaw?"

"Only by hearing that she and her brother are leading citizens of the city. If she recommends honey and tea I will certainly try that." He made his way out of the shop without having to buy any bread.

So, Benjamin Whitelaw was visiting his sister that night. That seemed harmless enough, but if he was close to his sister perhaps she would be the key to finding out more about him. After all, Daniel hadn't been warned to keep away from her.

CHAPTER TWENTY THREE

Charlotte Asks for Help

November 13, 1842.

All day Monday Charlotte wondered whether Daniel was having any luck finding out more about Mr. Whitelaw. As she listened to the children's lessons, she wandered often to the window to see whether he was coming down the road. When lessons were over she went to the kitchen. The only way to stop worrying about what was happening in Boston was to keep her hands busy. She volunteered to help the pie group make pumpkin pie. Smashing pumpkins worked off some of her restless energy.

The next day was almost as bad but when the mail came just before dinner Charlotte was pleased to see a letter from Daniel. Fanny, who was handing out the mail, looked at her curiously and said. "You are privileged to receive so many missives from that young newspaperman. Just remember we have serious work to do here and little time for flirtations and idleness."

Charlotte could have told her that there was a great deal of flirting and some idleness too at the Farm, but she only smiled and said, "Mr. Gallagher is a serious young man. You may be sure we are not flirting." She put the letter in her pocket and as soon as possible ran to her room to read it in peace.

Dear Miss Edgerton,

My luck has not been good today. I found my way to Mr. Whitelaw's stable but before I could get any information about his whereabouts, I was discovered as a reporter and ordered off the premises in no uncertain terms. I won't tax your patience with all my misadventures, but eventually Mr. Cabot informed me I will have only one more chance to solve the mystery of Reverend Hopewell's death or will sacrifice my chances of a permanent position on the newspaper.

Eventually I was able to return to the house that I saw Mr. Whitelaw enter last Thursday evening and finally discovered that it is the home of his sister Miss Tabitha Whitelaw. Perhaps she would be able to tell us something about her brother's whereabouts last month now that I cannot visit either Mr. Whitelaw's home or his office.

Do you suppose that through your friend Margaret Fuller you might be able to get an introduction to Miss Whitelaw and pay a call on her? I cannot think of another way we could get the information we so badly need.

Your respectful friend,

Daniel Gallagher

Charlotte carried the letter to class and through much of the afternoon her mind wandered to thoughts of how to ask Margaret Fuller for such a favor. She told herself she had no right to ask Miss Fuller to take such a great interest in her concerns, but "nothing ventured, nothing gained" as her mother used to say. If she were rebuffed, she and Daniel would just have to find some other way.

Charlotte remembered the eagerness in Daniel's voice every time he talked about being a newspaperman, and she sighed when she thought of him losing that chance forever. At last she screwed up her courage and plunged into writing a letter requesting the introduction.

On Friday she received a gracious note telling her to call on Miss Fuller at her home in Boston on Sunday. There she would be able to meet Miss Whitelaw. Charlotte quickly sent a line to Daniel to let him know about her success. She would have been happy to have him accompany her, but of course could not invite him to Miss Fuller's home. Besides, Miss Whitelaw might have heard Daniel's name from her brother. She would scarcely be pleased to meet a man who had so disturbed her brother and his family. She would have to pay the visit alone. Well, she'd often done things alone before and knew she could manage it.

The easiest way to get to Boston on a Sunday was to join whatever group was going there for church services. There were many at the Farm who enjoyed hearing a good sermon and would often travel quite a distance for Sunday services with a well-known preacher. Charlotte travelled with Fanny Gray and Abigail Pretlove who was taking Timothy to a special children's service where Bronson Alcott would be speaking. Everyone was cheerful as they bounced along in the carriage, but each had her own thoughts to ponder, so there was not much chatter on the trip. They parted at the edge of the Common to go their separate ways.

When Charlotte reached the Fuller house, she walked slowly up the steps and felt a tremor of shyness, but when she entered she found a warm welcome. Margaret Fuller introduced her to her mother, a gentle-looking white-haired woman sitting in a rocking chair near the fire. The three of them settled themselves in the comfortable chairs and after some polite conversation Mrs. Fuller excused herself and left.

Margaret Fuller turned to Charlotte, "How are you and Mr. Gallagher getting along in your efforts to find out how Reverend Hopewell died?"

Charlotte sighed and launched into a recital of the efforts they had made to discover what had happened. She had to admit that they had been unable to learn anything about Mr. Whitelaw's whereabouts on the night of Reverent Hopewell's death. Miss Fuller leaned forward, listening with interest as Charlotte talked about their disappointments.

"I am glad to say that I saw Miss Tabitha Whitelaw yesterday at a lecture we both attended and I have invited her here this afternoon so you will have an opportunity to talk with her."

Soon they heard a knock. Miss Fuller went to the door and came back with a tall, thin woman wearing a gray dress and cloak. A black velvet bonnet covered her gray-streaked dark hair. Miss Fuller introduced the two women and they exchanged polite chit-chat about the weather and the likelihood of snow while Charlotte tried desperately to find a way to introduce the questions she wanted to ask. She couldn't admit that she had met Miss Whitelaw's sister-in-law because she had done that under false pretenses. Instead she floundered on talking about Brook Farm and how much she enjoyed living there.

Margaret Fuller saved her by plunging into the substance of the questions. "I understand your brother is considering investing in Mr. Ripley's community. Have you ever thought about doing that yourself?"

"No, no, I am quite content in my own little house here in Boston and would not want to uproot myself for an experimental life, no matter how noble. I have several charities to which I devote my time and what little support I can give them. My brother has a wider world of claims on his attention. I am quite sure he would not choose to live at Brook Farm as you do, Miss Edgerton, but he might invest money in the enterprise. His wife has a wide circle of friends here in the city and entertains often in their beautiful home. I cannot imagine her wanting to live in a quiet rural community."

Did Charlotte detect a hint of displeasure in Tabitha's voice? She wasn't quite sure, but decided to dig deeper. "I have heard that Mrs. Whitelaw is a very attractive woman and quite a leader in society."

"Mrs. Whitelaw is indeed an attractive and charming young woman. She dotes on her two young sons, but they do not take up much of her time, so she does indeed do a great deal of entertaining."

"She must make their home a cheerful and lively place for your brother to come home to after his long days of work", Charlotte ventured daringly.

"I daresay she does," Tabitha responded somewhat tartly, "but I don't want to give the impression that his wife is flighty or frivolous. She is a faithful church member and never misses a sermon or a service at their church. She was especially impressed by the young Reverend Hopewell whose tragic fate has saddened us all."

"Was her husband also impressed by Reverend Hopewell? I have heard that he sometimes seemed to have more followers among the women of his congregation than the men."

Tabitha Whitelaw looked at Charlotte a bit sternly when she said that but her response was simply, "My brother is perhaps not quite as devoted a churchgoer as many of us women are, but he certainly was shaken by Reverend Hopewell's death. He is now on the congregational committee to find a new pastor."

There was a pause when Margaret Fuller left the room for a few moments and came back with a plate of biscuits. Her mother followed carrying a tray with tea and plates. Charlotte worried about Daniel and his concern about his position with Mr. Cabot, but Tabitha Whitelaw did not seem indiscreet enough to say anything that might reflect on her brother. This visit was not helping the search at all.

Tabitha began talking about her work with the Abolition Society and urged Margaret Fuller and Charlotte to turn their efforts to aiding the runaway slaves from the South who were increasingly coming to the city to find a route north to freedom. "We are building up an entire Underground Railroad of safe houses where farmers and others are willing to allow these people to stay during the day. They travel mostly by night making the way up to Fitchburg and then to Lake Champlain and so across the border to Canada. We would like to have the Brook Farmers participate with us in this attempt, but I am afraid the Ripleys are a bit too timid for the endeavor."

"It would be difficult to hide anyone in a community as crowded and as talkative as Brook Farm, wouldn't it?" asked Margaret Fuller. "I don't think there is any way of keeping a secret there because people are in and out of each other's business all the time."

"Surely they all support abolition, don't they?" asked Tabitha.

"The majority do," Charlotte assured her, "but there is no kind of bizarre belief that cannot be found at Brook Farm. Some of the students are from the South and I wonder whether they would feel it was their duty to return escaped slaves to their legal owners."

Tabitha looked horrified. "But all of Boston is united on the injustice of the Fugitive Slave Act. There has never yet been a slave returned to the South from Boston and there is unlikely to be one. Slavery is an evil that must be kept from spreading across the country. We have enough slave states as it is without expanding the reach of slaveholders."

"As Miss Edgerton says," Margaret Fuller joined in. "There are as many opinions at Brook Farm as there are people. I have heard from several acquaintances there that resettling the slaves in Africa or another colony is the only solution, while others call for immediate emancipation. I don't know that anyone is working on such practical details as how to help runaways."

"My friend Fanny Gray is deeply concerned about runaways, although I have not spoken to her about it in quite some time. My brother corresponded with her, I believe, and influenced her thinking on the subject."

Charlotte was surprised to hear that Fanny would have had the courage to correspond with a man about any subject. This was a link she would like to learn more about.

CHAPTER TWENTY FOUR

Abigail Remembers the Past

November 13, 1842.

Timothy was delighted with Bronson Alcott's conversation with the children. While the adults listened to a sermon in the church, the children were taken to the Parish Hall to for their own service. No matter how long-winded and ponderous in conversation with adults, Alcott was always successful in talking to children. They came bursting out of the Hall and into the vestry to meet their families after both services were finished.

"He asked us how we knew we had a soul," Timothy exclaimed excitedly to Abigail. "And he listened to everything anyone said."

"What did you tell him?" she asked.

"I told him I knew there was something inside me that made me happy when I did good things like saving that little bird I found on the grass this summer. Remember?" Abigail certainly did remember finding the bird fluttering under one of the apple trees. Timothy had run to get a stool from the barn and together they returned the bird to its nest on the lowest branch of the tree.

"What did Mr. Alcott say when you told him that?"

"He told me that was very good proof I had a soul. Then a lot of the other children started telling him about why they thought they had souls. I thought mine was the best though."

Timothy was inclined to boast and Abigail smiled apologetically at Fanny over his head. She was smiling too at the children's enthusiasm. It was impossible not to. Although she missed the silent Quaker services of her childhood, she had never found them as exciting as Timothy had found Bronson Alcott's talk.

Fanny and Abigail walked back to the stable to find the Brook Farm carriage. On the way back to Brook Farm they talked about the sermon they had heard. It had not been inspiring.

"Why are some ministers so much more gifted in preaching than others?" Abigail wondered. "Don't they all learn to preach in Divinity School?"

"It is not always the way they preach that makes a minister popular with his congregation," Fanny retorted. "Fine looking ministers often charm their listeners no matter what they say or how well they preach."

"It certainly is easier to pay attention to a handsome man in the pulpit," Abigail agreed "than to a dried up stick of a man who mumbles his sermon. There have been many Sundays when I have listened to a sermon and scarcely remembered a word of it. You are probably far too devout to worry about the preacher's good looks."

"I am not blind," Fanny replied rather bitterly. "I too appreciate having an attractive man of God to inspire us, but I try to pay attention only to the message. Some ministers allow themselves to be too flattered by the response and admiration of their congregation, especially the women who fawn over them. I am sometimes afraid that our friend the Reverend Hopewell had a weakness in this area. His injudicious behavior led to distrust among some of the men who were originally his staunch supporters."

Abigail was shocked into silence by that outpouring. For the past month she had heard nothing but kind words about Winslow and sorrow about his terrible death. No matter how angry she had sometimes been at him, she had never doubted that his behavior toward his congregation was everything it should have been.

"Surely you misjudge him," she finally said. "I have heard nothing but praise of his work and his success in ministering to his flock."

"Perhaps you have not heard all that has been said," Fanny retorted darkly. Her forehead creased into a frown as she continued. "I myself know that certain men in his congregation were questioning his behavior. There was even some consideration given to asking him to find a new pulpit rather than staying at the Third Street Church." She subsided into silence with a grim shrug.

Abigail leaned back into the carriage cushion and retreated into her own thoughts. During those few conversations she had had with Winslow in the days after he appeared at Brook Farm, they had not talked much about his work, but he had touched upon it. What was it he said about "foolish women" in his congregation? Something about an unmarried minister being at the mercy of women who were dissatisfied with their lives and wanted someone to listen to their every thought and feeling. He certainly never said that some of the men were annoyed with him or dissatisfied with his preaching. But had he suggested that possibility? Why had she not paid more attention?

Timothy was dozing off in the carriage as the horse clip-clopped along the muddy road. Fanny suddenly interrupted Abigail's thoughts by saying, "You pay no attention to me. Few people do, but

I know many secrets the rest of you never suspect. You may say that Winslow Hopewell's behavior was above reproach, but my friend Tabitha Whitelaw has told me that her brother was sure Reverend Hopewell was improperly addressing his wife. She had made a habit of going to the parsonage for private conversations with him and fussed and preened as though she were going to a ball. You can't tell me their relationship was not beyond that which a minister should have with a married woman. Besides, the Reverend Hopewell was by no means perfect in other matters either. He had promised George Ripley he would invest in the Community, but then at the last moment withdrew his support without an excuse of any kind." Fanny's voice was shrill.

Timothy woke with a start and looked around with a worried frown. "What's wrong, Mama?" he asked. Abigail tried to soothe him and gave no reply to Fanny. Fortunately the carriage was just pulling up at Brook Farm so the silence went unremarked.

A tall woman in a dark dress was striding across the lawn from the barn to the kitchen door. Abigail recognized the colored woman who had attended Lydia Maria Child's talk weeks before. Fanny looked surprised and her face softened. She smiled and waved at the woman. "I have some business to attend to," she said to Abigail as she walked to meet the woman.

Later that afternoon Abigail went down to the parlor and joined the small group listening to the soothing music John Dwight was playing. Timothy sat and listened for a while and then wandered off with his friends. A fire was burning in the fireplace and she hoped the gentle tones of the piano would take her mind off Winslow Hopewell. He had been an imperfect man, but surely he had never done anything to justify intense jealousy. She remembered how earnest he had looked the last time she spoke to him and his serious voice when he told her he was trying to make amends for the sins and errors of his youth. Surely a man who was so thoughtful and sincere could not have acted improperly with another man's wife.

Lost in her thoughts, she was jolted by hearing someone ask Charles Dana, "Is it true that you are leaving us? We will miss you and the students will lose the lessons that have taught."

"Surely you are not leaving!" Abigail exclaimed without thinking. "You've been a part of the community since the beginning. How will the children manage without their lessons? What is it you are leaving us for?"

Poor Charles Dana looked uncomfortable, his pale cheeks flushed and he ran his fingers through his blond hair before he answered in a low voice. "It is by no means certain yet that I will go. As you say, I have been active in the Community since its beginning. But I am a man without money and I would like to get married. How can I ask a woman to share her life with me when I cannot even pay off the debts I already have?"

"But when our community is more successful and our membership grows, there will be income from the farm and from the school will there not?" Abigail persisted. "The members will share in those benefits I believe. Perhaps you will have enough to pay your debts."

"I have been living on that hope for the past two years," Dana replied. "It's hard to keep faith in the promise of rewards when both the school and the farm are struggling. But let's not worry about that today. John is about to play another piece and perhaps Mozart will cheer us all."

While Abigail was listening, she saw Charlotte come into the room. Her face was rosy from being out in the air and she took a seat close to the fire. When the music was over, the others left the room and Charlotte and Abigail were left alone. Charlotte told Abigail about her visit with Margaret Fuller and her meeting with Tabitha Whitelaw.

"What is she like?" Abigail asked, wondering whether she was one of the women who admired Winslow so much.

"She seems very austere and reserved," answered Charlotte. "She's a no-nonsense woman who is devoted to the cause of abolition. She expressed regret about Reverend Hopewell's death but I think her brother and his wife were more active members of the church than she was. Her sister-in-law, Violet Whitelaw, in particular was apparently distraught about his death."

Abigail felt a twinge of jealousy as she wondered whether Winslow had been attracted to this woman. What right had she to be distraught about his death?

Charlotte was looking gloomy. "I'm afraid I haven't discovered anything that will get us closer to the answer about how Reverend Hopewell died," she admitted. "Mr. Whitelaw might indeed have been jealous and very angry about his supposed behavior, but was he here on the day of the death? Neither Mr. Gallagher nor I have been able to find out what he was doing that morning."

"Do you suppose he could have sent someone else to commit the crime? Seamen are not always known as God-fearing and virtuous men. Perhaps he sent someone else to warn Reverend Hopewell to stay away from his wife. That could have led to a fight and the dreadful end of it."

Charlotte's eyes widened. "I hadn't thought about that possibility. I suppose Mr. Whitelaw might have sent someone else. What made you think of such a thing?"

"Wasn't that the way Mary Queen of Scot's husband was killed? Her lover didn't do the deed himself; he persuaded others to commit the act. When you look back in history so many deaths were caused by jealous husbands and lovers. Of course Winslow was not a wicked Scottish lord or anything like that, but strange and wicked things happen even in Massachusetts."

"Where does that leave us in our search? How can we possibly find out whether Benjamin Whitelaw had done something so vile?" Charlotte's head drooped as she thought of the impossible task.

Abigail could not think of any way to track all of Whitelaw's movements in the days leading up to Winslow's death. He would have talked with many of his employees and seamen, especially the officers who commanded his ships. There was no way to know what he told them or whether he requested their help in confronting Winslow.

"I guess we have to go back to asking people whether any stranger was seen around the Farm that day." Charlotte sighed as she said it. "Surely no one in our community would have failed to report a stranger, but how did the man travel from Boston? Perhaps one of the farmers along the road saw something. We have a long task ahead of us."

CHAPTER TWENTY FIVE

Daniel Looks for Work

November 14, 1842.

Monday morning lay ahead of Daniel, a gloomy stretch of dead time and not much chance of getting anything done. It reminded him of days at home when the fish weren't running and the surf too high to take out a boat. Nothing to do but kick the rocks along the shore and wonder where the money would come from to buy this evening's meal. Too many of these days and a man could lose all hope. Last week he had been dreaming of winning glory by solving the crime and writing it up. He could see himself showing Charlotte the newspaper and telling her Mr. Cabot was hiring him to be his star reporter. Stupid dreams...like a child dreaming of sugarplums.

He needed money, so he had to find work. The last few weeks he had spent some time at the Court House writing stories for Mr. Cabot. Maybe he could work there. He could do a clerk's job thanks to the good hand Father Sheehan taught him night after night at the rectory. The priest had driven him like a slave, but it was worth it in the end.

The Court House was no more welcoming than it had been before. The usual crowd of lawyers and merchants who cluttered the lobby begrudged Daniel the space to walk through. Upstairs was quieter. He stopped in Judge Adams's antechamber but the head clerk took one look at him and said they needed no help. It was just as Mrs. Costello had told him, "You've got the map of Ireland on your face and most of these Yankees would rather hire the Devil himself than an Irishman."

When he got to Sheriff Grover's office, Daniel found the sheriff berating the one clerk who was there. "Where are the records of the deeds from the orchards up near Dedham? I told you last week that I'd need those by Monday."

"I've been doing the copying for days, sir," the clerk answered in a timid voice, "but Charles has gone to Maine to visit his dying mother and I cannot get all the deeds copied myself. I'm working as fast as I can. I promise you'll have them in the morning even if I have to work all night."

"The morning's not good enough," fumed the Sheriff. "They have to be ready for Mr. Whitelaw when he comes in right after dinner. It won't do me any good to have you still scratching away with your pen when he arrives."

"Perhaps I can help," Daniel piped up. "I could start working right away and help with the copying. I've a fair hand and I'm quick."

Before he knew it he was sitting at the clerk's high desk with a stack of deeds in front of him. Copying the deeds was dull work, but Daniel looked forward to having a few coins in his pocket at the end of the day. Maybe if Charles was away all week he'd earn enough to keep him in food for a while so he could continue his investigation.

By dinnertime Josiah and Daniel had finished the orchard deeds the Sheriff was so worried about. The sheriff was pleased with Daniel's work and told him to come back after dinner to copy some other papers. He and Josiah walked over to a nearby tavern where he bought a half-penny's worth of fried potatoes and Josiah had a slice of kidney pie. Daniel asked him if he knew Mr. Whitelaw or had ever seen him before.

"Oh, indeed I've seen him. He comes in quite often because he owns a lot of land around the city and he is always buying and selling. He's a jolly enough man if you don't cross him, but whew! What a temper he has if you do. I've seen him get angry even at the sheriff over some delay in his blasted deeds."

Every word Daniel heard made it sound more likely that Whitelaw could be a killer. He wondered what the reaction would be if Whitelaw found him working in the sheriff's office. He'd just have to keep his head down and hope for the best. Soon after he returned with Josiah to the office Daniel had a chance to see Whitelaw in action.

The sheriff was sitting at his desk going over some papers that had arrived by messenger, when there was the sound of loud footsteps on the stairs. The door swung open and Mr. Whitelaw came storming in. Did he always cause such a ruckus like a thunderstorm breaking hard on everyone in its path?

"Do you have my deeds, sheriff?" he asked walking toward the desk. When the sheriff assured him the deeds were ready, he drew a chair up to the desk and sat down.

Daniel was out of his line of vision the way he was sitting, but what if he moved and looked around? On coming in Whitelaw had looked at no one but the sheriff and seemed scarcely aware there were clerks in the room. Now he was talking to the sheriff in a low voice, oblivious to everyone around him.

Finally he stood up and said in a louder voice. "Well, I'll leave it to you then. I'll be away for several weeks starting a week Monday. I'm having trouble with some of my customers in New York. Last month I was down there for weeks. Didn't get back until mid-October. I might as well start my own factory here in Boston if those people can't learn to make proper oil lamps that can use our high quality whale oil. I'll come in to see you when I return."

With that he turned to leave and his eye swept over the clerks sitting on on their high stools. Daniel looked down at his desk as if he was working very hard, but he could feel Whitelaw's eyes on him and thought for a breathless moment that he paused.

Finally, Whitelaw turned and hurried out the door, clattering down the stairs just as he had come in. It was a close call, but Daniel had escaped a scolding and given the sheriff no reason to throw him out.

Not that his troubles were over. "Several weeks" Whitelaw had said "not back until mid-October" it sounded as though he wasn't anywhere near Boston much less Brook Farm when Winslow Hopewell met his fate. What did that do to all their clever ideas? If he had been in New York he couldn't be blamed, but if he was not guilty then who was?

Daniel had been so sure he'd found the culprit at last that he hadn't let himself doubt it was just a matter of proving Whitelaw had been out to the Farm that fatal morning. Now it seemed Whitelaw could not have been there. With a sigh, Daniel dipped his pen into the ink and went back to copying documents again.

When the light disappeared from the sky, Josiah found an oil lamp to work by, although the flickering light was unfriendly to the eye. At last Sheriff Grover told them they could leave. He gave Daniel a few coins and told him to come back the next day because there was a backlog of documents that needed copying. It looked as though he might have a job for as long as Charles stayed in Maine with his mother.

Dejectedly Daniel walked back to the boarding house. He was glad he had found work, but it was not what he had dreamed of. What he really wanted to do was to solve the mystery of Reverend Hopewell's death, write a story that would impress Mr. Cabot, and become a regular member of the newspaper staff.

Mrs. Costello had kept some of her stew hot on the stove for him. The stew warmed him and made him feel more cheerful, but finding a letter from Charlotte waiting for him was even better.

Dear Mr. Gallagher,

I regret to tell you that my efforts have not been very helpful, but I have had several most interesting conversations. I talked with Tabitha Whitelaw who confirmed our belief that her sister-in-law is a bit frivolous and that her brother could well be jealous. She did not say this in so many words, but the tone of what she said left that strong impression on me. However, she gave no information about where her brother might have been at the time of Reverend Hopewell's death, so we are no closer to having any proof of foul play.

When I returned to Brook Farm I also talked with Abigail who had significant news. She told me that she drove home from church with Fanny Gray who talked eagerly about troubles at the Third Street Church and her belief that there was at least one jealous man in the congregation. Abigail also suggested to me that perhaps Mr. Whitelaw would not have had to be at the Farm himself but could have sent someone else to warn Reverend Hopewell to stay away from his wife.

These are troubling thoughts and I am eager to talk them over with you. Perhaps you could come out to the Farm on Wednesday afternoon if you do not have other work or perhaps next Sunday.

Cordially,

Charlotte Edgerton

Charlotte's letter gave Daniel a new idea. He had not considered the possibility that Benjamin Whitelaw might have sent someone else to talk with Hopewell, or possibly to threaten him. But how could he discover who it might be? If he had to investigate all of the officers and men who worked on the Whitelaw ships, it would take months. Some of them might have sailed after the crime was committed and would by now be far off in the Southern seas. Whaling trips often lasted for years. He and Charlotte would never be able to track all the men down.

He went up to his room and paced up and down the small space trying to think. The very walls of the room, mustardy yellow with a few brown streaks where water had leaked in around the tiny window, reminded him of illness. He'd seen the yellow faces of folks with jaundice that was slowly killing them. But he wasn't going to think such gloomy thoughts. He was going to make a new life in this new country and somehow he would find a way to win back Mr. Cabot's respect.

They needed to find someone who had been out in the early morning when Reverend Hopewell was taking his walk. There were good reasons for many people to be up before dawn during the short autumn days to attend to chores especially on a farm. Abner Platt had been there; that's how he had seen Rory O'Connor. He jumped to the conclusion that Rory was the murderer, but there must have been someone else out that morning. Platt might not have even noticed someone else because his first thought was that an Irish tramp must have been guilty. What if he was so eager to blame the crime on Rory that he neglected to mention anyone else he had seen? Perhaps if Daniel went back and questioned him there would be more to learn. And that wasn't all. What about Rory? Daniel spread out a piece of paper and added a few drops of water from the shaving pitcher to his precious small jar of ink.

Dear Miss Edgerton,

Thank you for your letter and your sensible idea that someone might have acted for Benjamin Whitelaw. This is important because I learned today that Mr. Whitelaw was traveling to New York at the time of the Reverend Hopewell's death. We must find out whether he might have had an accomplice working with him.

Our task now is to discover whether anyone saw a stranger around the Farm on the morning of the death. Perhaps you could interview Mr. and Mrs. Platt. They might have more information than they have given us so far. I am afraid I was clumsy when I asked questions at the Platt farm and may have learned less than I could have done if I had been more diplomatic.

As for me, I have found work in the sheriff's office replacing a clerk who is visiting his mother. I will have to continue to work there for the rest of this week because I must pay my board and expenses. However I will seek out Rory O'Connor and question him about whether there might have been any other person lurking about the Brook Farm property that morning.

My time will not be my own for the rest of this week, but I will visit you on next Sunday and we can compare the information we have learned. You can be assured I will be thinking of you and wishing you well for the remainder of the week.

Your respectful and affectionate friend,

Daniel Gallagher

CHAPTER TWENTY SIX

Charlotte Talks to a Farm Wife

November 16, 1842.

Charlotte waited eagerly for Daniel's letter, but was sharply disappointed when it arrived. So Benjamin Whitelaw was nowhere near Brook Farm when Winslow died—what did that mean? She had been sure he was the man responsible. Violet Whitelaw was a weak, silly woman. Charlotte could understand why listening to her talk about her interest in the minister might lead her husband to do something he would regret. She had heard stories enough about matrons in some of the fashionable parishes who somehow confused their adoration of the Deity with their admiration of his servant in the pulpit.

Daniel's suggestion to talk with Abner Platt and his wife Hetty made sense. Daniel had aroused Mr. Platt's anger by his attempt to spy on the barn, but perhaps she could approach Mrs. Platt. She might not have been quite so annoyed by the suspicions of outsiders because no one had questioned her yet. Like all farm wives she would have been up before dawn, so perhaps she saw someone in the area but never thought to mention it. Charlotte resolved to visit her after dinner on Wednesday, when she would have time to sit and talk for a few minutes.

Wednesday morning went slowly as Charlotte helped her students with their struggle to learn to read. They were copying a short verse from their primer. Timothy, as usual, was the first student to finish his lesson and he proudly presented his slate with every word copied correctly and clearly. Charlotte thought of how proud his father would have been of him if only he had been spared and tears stung her eyes. She was more determined than ever to find out what had happened.

When the morning finally ended Charlotte led her charges down to dinner and watched to see that they all were silent and attentive during grace. After that she was free to enjoy her own dinner and enjoy every mouthful of the delicious pork and beans. It was no trouble to join the cleaning crew afterward and help clear the tables. One of the things she liked most about Brook Farm was the way everyone helped with chores without complaining. She thought, as she often did, that the Ripleys had devised a fine scheme for living, although not many people in the outside world seemed inclined to join.

After dinner she slipped on a warm cloak and started toward Mr. Platt's farm. The weather had turned very cold this week. Snow threatened every day, but so far had produced only a few short snow showers that ended almost as soon as they began. Not a soul was on the road as she walked up a barely-marked path to the weather-beaten farmhouse. Behind the house was a large vegetable patch barren now except for a couple of languishing pumpkins too small to bother harvesting.

The kitchen door was closed tight against the wind, but Charlotte knocked sharply and heard a child's voice cry out "Someone's at the door". A minute later the door opened to reveal a sturdy woman wearing a dark blue dress and red-checked apron. Her blonde hair made her face look youthful even though it was graying at the temples. Behind her the kitchen was warm and fragrant from a large kettle of soup bubbling on the stove.

"Good afternoon," she said. "You are one of the young ladies from Brook Farm, aren't you?"

"Yes, I am, Mrs. Platt. My name is Charlotte Edgerton and I am a member of the Community. I teach the young children there, children about the age of your son here." Charlotte stepped inside the kitchen and enjoyed the welcoming warmth. "I wonder if I could talk to you for a few minutes about the recent unfortunate events at the Farm."

Mrs. Platt invited her to sit at the large wooden table and insisted on making tea. While they talked she busily peeled and diced potatoes for the soup. Her son quietly played with the potato peels pushing and pulling them around the table and twisting them into figures like stick men.

Charlotte scarcely knew how to begin, but she plunged in. "You have no doubt heard that one of the guests who was visiting the Farm was struck down early one morning several weeks ago. I know your husband was out early that morning and saw a man on the road that he thought might have been responsible. As it turned out the sheriff decided that man was not involved."

"Yes, I know all that," Mrs. Platt said in a gentle, plaintive voice. "That's what the sheriff told Abner, although he still isn't sure that the Irishman wasn't to blame. He said to me, 'Hetty, the good people at Brook Farm aren't going about hurting one another. If it's not the tramp then who could it be?' and I have to agree the Irishman seems the most likely."

"Were you out early that morning, too?" Charlotte asked. "Did you see the Irishman or anyone else about?"

Hetty Platt considered this seriously before she answered. "I went out early to feed the chickens just like I do every morning. You should hear the racket that rooster makes waking us all up before dawn. We couldn't sleep late even if we had a mind to." She stopped for a minute to put a bowl full of potatoes into the soup kettle. Then she came back and started peeling more.

"It was a foggy morning as I recall and I couldn't see as far as the other side of the road. When I walked toward the chicken coop, I heard a noise across the way. A few yelps like a dog was being disturbed and of course their roosters started crowing too, same as ours. I saw one figure—a man—walking toward the patch of trees beside the barn. Later I thought that must have been Reverend Hopewell. It makes me shiver to think of it."

"But you didn't see anyone else?" Charlotte leaned across the table eager to catch every word.

"The sun was just coming up and I was busy with those chickens. I heard the baby start crying here in the house and I wanted to get back to tend to him. I scarcely paid the Brook Farm place any attention. They do things differently there. Those folks do their farming any time of day and they don't seem to think much of real farmers like us."

Charlotte could hear the grievance in her voice, but didn't want to say anything take her away from her memories of what happened that morning.

Finally she continued, "I looked over at the Community a couple of times, wondering what that man was doing walking into the woods. And I kinda thought I saw someone else. Might have been a woman, but why would a woman be out there at that hour? There's no chickens in that patch of woods."

A woman! That wasn't what Charlotte had expected to hear. Why would a woman have walked out there so early in the morning? Benjamin Whitelaw would never in the world have sent a woman to pick a quarrel with Reverend Hopewell. It made no sense at all.

"Do you think it might have been a man wearing a cape or something like that?" she asked.

"I've never seen a man in a long skirt, but as I say the morning was foggy and I wasn't paying all that much attention. I have my own family to take care of not to mention the chickens. I don't have time to pry into other people's business. I wasn't snooping."

"Oh, of course not. I understand that. Probably there was nothing at all to see. I didn't mean to bother you. You are a busy woman and you have a lot of work to do here."

Mrs. Platt had finished peeling her potatoes now and was putting the peels into a bucket. No doubt their pigs would feast on those. The little boy was sorry to lose his playthings and was pulling on his mother's skirt saying, "An apple. I want an apple?" It was time to go back to Brook Farm.

Back at the Farm she settled down in the parlor to read one of the books Mr. Ripley made available for everyone. She was tired of trying to solve problems that had no answers. Fanny was sitting at the desk on the other side of the room writing, probably a letter to her brother. Charlotte had scarcely started reading before Abigail came in with Timothy. He wanted to look at some of the books too and chose one with pictures of insects and fish. He lay down on the floor and soon was poring over it while Abigail sat in front of the fire knitting winter mittens for him.

Charlotte soon began to tell Abigail about her visit with Hetty Platt. "I had hoped she might be able to remember seeing someone who had been in the area on the night that Reverend Hopewell died. She was friendly enough and tried to help, but I'm afraid she didn't see very much."

"It was very early in the morning," Abigail agreed. "It would be difficult to see people across the road and the lawn that lies between here and the Platt house."

"Mrs. Platt said she thought she saw a figure moving among the trees. That must have been Reverend Hopewell. Then she added that she might have seen another figure—a woman—but that that seems unlikely. How would a woman find her way out here at such an early hour? And why would she come? I suggested it might have been a man in a long cloak, but Mrs. Platt did not really agree."

"A man in a long cloak sounds a bit fanciful. Most likely Mrs. Platt did not see a figure at all, perhaps just a bush blowing in the wind or even an animal. Deer sometimes come down toward the trees early in the morning to forage."

"It's not easy to mistake a deer for a woman," Charlotte insisted. "Perhaps Mrs. Platt saw nothing but a bush blowing in the wind, but there must have been someone about in those woods. Someone who was willing to injure Reverend Hopewell."

A clatter across the room interrupted their talk. Fanny had stopped writing and stood up abruptly knocking her chair to the floor. Timothy ran over to help her right it, but Fanny didn't even thank the child as she left the room. Abigail made up for the lack by giving Timothy a hug and a kiss and telling him he was a good boy.

"Fanny certainly seems upset," Charlotte commented. "Do you think we were making too much noise with our talk? Or maybe that's just Fanny being cross again."

"Don't be angry at Fanny. She's been on edge ever since this terrible thing happened," Abigail reminded her gently. "I think everyone at Brook Farm has suffered and no one knows what to do. We all have questions and no answers." Her voice hovered on the edge of tears and Timothy moved closer to lean against his mother's shoulder.

Charlotte had no answer to that and the evening ended on a gloomy note.

CHAPTER TWENTY SEVEN

Daniel Asks More Questions

November 19, 1842.

Daniel worked all week for the sheriff. It wasn't until Saturday afternoon when the office closed that he finally had a chance to track down Rory O'Connor. Last month when he had looked, Rory turned up in no time working on the docks, but this time Daniel couldn't find anyone who had seen him. A light snow started falling as he tramped the streets and he was soon chilled to the bone. The light was fading over the docks and everyone had stopped working.

Finally he stopped in a small tavern close to the docks to warm up. A steaming pot of oyster stew was bubbling on the stove and he was glad to buy a bowl. The landlord's wife, who was in charge of the stew, was friendly, so Daniel plied her with questions about Rory.

"I'm looking for a friend named Rory O'Connor. Do you have any idea where I might find him?"

"Is he a Kerry man?" she asked. "That's my county and I knew an O'Connor family came here from Kerry when my husband and I did, about ten years ago. But I think they headed West and I never heard from them."

"The Rory O'Connor I knew is from Galway. Kinvara I think. He might have signed on to a fishing vessel is what I'm thinking."

A few new customers came into the tavern calling for food and drink, so the landlady moved on to serving them and Daniel sat down at a table against the back wall. It wasn't easy to be patient when he was having so little luck. He should have asked Rory where he was living so he could find him again. He wanted desperately to have some news to give Charlotte when he saw her on Sunday.

His heart was slipping down into his boots as his mother would have said, while he slurped the oyster stew, but when he looked up who did he see but the very man he was looking for, Rory O'Connor. Maybe his luck was turning!

He jumped up and grabbed Rory's arm, "I'll stand you a treat, Rory, if you'll sit down and talk to me about what you saw out at Brook Farm."

Soon they were sitting together over pints of ale and bowls of stew and Rory was telling him again about the day he walked past the Platt farm and saw the group of people standing around in the wood.

"As I walked down the road, the sun was just coming up and that patch of woods looked dim and misty in the fog. I was moving slow and easy. I didn't want to be seen or heard. When you're wandering around a strange neighborhood, sleeping where maybe you're not welcome, and picking up any food that someone's carelessly left lying about, people can think you're a tramp. These Yankee farmers mostly think we're all tramps anyway. The minute I open my mouth I can see them reach for their purses as if they're afraid I'll snatch anything I can get.

"Anyway, I came down the road kind of cautious and slow, wondering why someone would be moving in the wood at this early hour. Strangest of all, it looked like someone in a long skirt—a woman, or maybe a priest in a cassock. Then the figure disappeared and I figured it was safe to move along a bit faster, but next thing I knew I saw another woman over there, a woman in a white dress that stood out against the trees. And then I heard a scream and the woman ran and people started running toward her—another woman and several men. I hid in a bush to see what was going on. Pretty soon there was a whole bunch of them standing around and talking, looking at something on the ground. I crept up closer to see what was going on. That's when I stopped behind that big bush they call the chokecherry. Then, like I told the sheriff, they weren't paying me no mind so I thought I'd skedaddle out of there and that's what I did."

"Would you tell the sheriff that whole story if he asks you about it?"

Rory nodded. "You're sure he's not thinking of arresting me again?"

"Not a chance." Daniel took out the paper and pencil he always carried. "Give me the address of your boarding house so I can find you if I need you again."

On Sunday when Daniel started out for Brook Farm the snow was starting to fall again, but not enough to bother him as he walked. The fields looked white and clean after having been brown and dying these past weeks. It made him think of a body laid out in a clean white winding sheet after being dressed in rags and dying in a foul hole of a room. Death can look a lot cleaner and purer than life, especially for poor people who spend their lives in hovels.

While he walked Daniel wondered what to make of Rory's story. He'd been hoping Rory would have seen someone Mr. Whitelaw might have sent out to the Farm. A man to pick a fight with Winslow or to lay down the law to him. Either way he would have chosen a good strong man to deliver his message, certainly not a woman. Maybe Rory was dreaming when he thought he saw a woman. At least the first woman. The woman in white who screamed must have been Abigail, but she ran off to get other people. She wasn't trying to hide anything. Was there a second woman? Did she really exist?

Charlotte was waiting when he got to the Farm. "I was afraid you weren't coming," she said. "They say this snow might bring a blizzard."

"A little snow can't keep me away," bragged Daniel. Charlotte gave him a sharp look and smiled as they went into the parlor.

"Did you have a chance to talk to Mr. Platt?" Daniel asked. "What did he have to say?"

"It was his wife I talked to. She was out early that day and saw part of what happened at the Farm. At least she thinks she did. She said it was a foggy morning and the light was dim, but she thought she saw someone. I don't know what to make of it because she thought it might be a woman—or a man in a long cloak—whoever she saw was wearing something that looked like a skirt. That can't be right, can it?"

Daniel jumped out of his chair and walked to the window when he heard that. "But that's what Rory said too. He said he thought he saw a woman in among the trees. And it wasn't Abigail, because he saw her in her white dress coming later and then screaming and bringing all the other people out. Is it possible there was a woman? If both Mrs. Platt and Rory saw someone, there must be something to it."

"Could a woman have killed Reverend Hopewell?" Charlotte looked unconvinced.

"A strong woman could have. It wouldn't be so difficult," Daniel pointed out. "Someone hit Hopewell with a hoe and he fell. It could have been the fall that killed him. Lots of women are strong—they work on farms and handle cattle. All sorts of things."

"That's true," Charlotte admitted. "I've known women who could outfight most men. How can we find out who the woman might be?" Charlotte frowned. "First we should ask Abigail more. It's very important that we find out everything she saw that morning." She jumped up from her chair, "I'll go get her."

She was back in a few minutes with Abigail, who sank down into a chair with a worried look. Charlotte remained standing. "Did you see anyone else nearby when you found Winslow Hopewell?" she asked.

"No, I didn't see anyone there. Of course I was so confused and shocked I scarcely noticed anything," Abigail replied slowly, twisting a corner of her skirt in her fingers.

"When you screamed and people came running to help you that morning," Daniel asked, "Who were the first people there?"

"Let's see. Two or three people came and stared at Winslow lying on the ground. And then George Ripley was there and he put his arm around my shoulder and led me over to his wife. She took me back to the house. I was crying. I could scarcely see by that time."

Charlotte gently took Abigail's hand, "Can you remember who was there before George Ripley came?"

Abigail brought her hands to her face to cover her eyes as though she was trying to visualize the scene. "Let's see, Fanny was there and Fred rushed up with Mrs. Geary following him. Then George Ripley and other people and as I said, he led me away to Sophia Ripley and she and I came back here. Oh, I don't want to think about it anymore tonight. I've gone over it so often in my mind."

Abigail slipped out of the room and Daniel and Charlotte were left staring at one another trying to take in what she had said. Finally Charlotte spoke. "Why is Fanny always there? Why was she so angry at Winslow Hopewell? Remember what she said about him not investing in the Farm even though he had promised? You don't suppose she could have done it, do you?"

Daniel didn't know what to think. The idea of a woman being responsible hadn't really occurred to him before today. It seemed impossible. Charlotte started speaking slowly, thinking as she went. "Fanny's a tall strong woman who never has trouble keeping up with the men. She carries pails of milk back and forth to the kitchen as though they're nothing. And I've seen her chopping away at dead stumps clearing the fields for planting as well as any man—chopping with a hoe." She stopped talking and sat looking at the floor.

"You know," she continued, "I think it might have been Fanny. She could have done it and she was so worried about the Farm and whether it was going to succeed. She was half out of her mind with worry sometimes. Maybe it was an accident and she just happened upon Reverend Hopewell and confronted him with what she thought was treachery. One thing could have led to another and..." Her voice trailed off and then she continued. "When she realized what happened, she would have been shocked and hardly have known what she was doing. I don't suppose she ever would have believed that she could do anything like that. She must have been terrified."

"But what do we do now?" Daniel asked. "We have no proof and we can't accuse her of anything. How can we be sure?"

"I'll talk to her," said Charlotte slowly. "Maybe there is some explanation."

Just then the parlor door opened and Fanny came in carrying a book.

Charlotte turned to her and quietly asked, "Fanny, why were you out in the woods?" She paused and drew her breath in sharply, trying to gather the courage to ask the question. "Why were you in the woods the morning Winslow Hopewell was found dead?"

Fanny looked stricken. Her pallid cheeks reddened. "You'd never understand! You don't understand anything." She turned abruptly and fled out of the room.

Once again Charlotte and Daniel were left staring speechlessly at one another.

CHAPTER TWENTY EIGHT

Fanny Speaks Out

November 20, 1842.

Fanny ran upstairs to her quiet bedroom and threw herself on the bed. Charlotte and Daniel's questioning eyes seemed to follow her there. She had to think but her mind was churning with memories and images. Words beat in her brain. Her restless mind kept talking on and on…

"No one ever listens to me! All my life I've been the quiet daughter in the corner doing everything my father and my brothers wanted of me. My mother kept me busy working in the kitchen while the boys stayed in the parlor listening to the men talk—laughing and arguing and calling for more food. I scurried around with platters of lamb and bowls of beans like a servant."

She jumped up from the bed and started pacing back and forth, but the words still pounded in her mind. "Father was proud of letting his sons speak up. When the war with the British started and recruiters came through asking young men to join the army to invade Lower Canada, he let John and Thomas speak up in front of the whole town and join the expedition. Mother warned them that war was not a game and they might be hurt, but no one listened.

"And when Thomas came back with his thigh all torn apart by a lucky shot from a British soldier, it was my mother and me who sat up all night with him tending the wound and keeping it clean. It was a glorious victory, my father said, but he didn't stay around and listen to Thomas moaning all night with an infected wound. Pus blossoming out no matter how often we cleaned the gaping wound. To this day Thomas walks with a limp and can scarcely ride a horse at all.

"It was that wound that killed Mother. Those nights the two of us sat up praying, and wiping Thomas's forehead and boiling more water for bandages to draw the pus out. Mother was never strong and those nights made her cough turn into a constant hacking. Father never seemed to notice even though he was a doctor. He should have known, but he was so busy at the Court House talking with the men about customs duties and taxes and which ships were being seized. He was more interested in the war than in taking care of his patients.

"Fanny help me," Mother would say as she weakened. Father and the boys weren't even there the day she died, lying on that white bed gasping for breath. It was only the cook and the parlor maid came up to sit by her for those last hours. And me at 15 left with a grown man and three hulking youths to take care of and a house to run.

"The boys moved out one by one. Their wives were all pretty girls, but flighty. First George, then Thomas and John. And I was left to take care of Father and keep house. He sent me to school. That's where I met Sophia Ripley and thank goodness for that. She was my only friend. We used to walk to school together and talk about everything under the sun. But there was no talking at home. Or if I did talk Father never bothered to listen to me. He taught me how to set a bone and how to make a poultice to draw the pus from a wound, but he never explained anything. What was the use of teaching a girl?

"And when he got older and had the fit that laid him low, it wasn't me he called on. It was my mother, calling her all the time he was lying in bed wandering in his head—Mary, Mary, Mary—in his feeble voice. But I was the one who took care of him. Not his beautiful Mary. She was gone. He was left with only plain Fanny and I don't think he ever got used to that."

That was all over years ago. Fanny struggled to turn off the voice in her head. Now there was a letter to be written. Sophia would understand why she had to leave despite all their dreams. Sophia was the only one who ever listened. Fanny had been so lonely after her father died, even with the house and the income he left. When George and Sophia decided to start this Community where everyone would work together and live together, it sounded like heaven on earth. And it could have been if only people had kept their promises. No one understood how important that was. And no one ever listened. The letter must be written right away. It was time to leave.

Dearest Sophia,

You will be astonished by what I am about to tell you, but I hope you will read this letter to the end and perhaps you will understand why I am leaving. And perhaps you will be able to forgive at least some of my sins. I never meant to do anything wrong. I wanted so much to help you and your devoted husband. The Brook Farm Community, as you must know, was the dearest dream of my life. I was honored to be able to invest in the Community and to be a part of it.. I poured all of my money into the venture despite the advice of my brother Thomas who wanted me to preserve my money for myself until the Community had proven itself to be successful.

I did not listen to Thomas. I prayed to God and believed He answered my prayer telling me to join my fortunes with you and move out here to West Roxbury to build a new world. But if God answered my prayer, He evidently did not answer everyone else's prayer and tell them to invest in the Farm. One by one the faithful have fallen away. Nathaniel Hawthorne came to join us but stayed only a few months. He said he needed solitude to work at his art and to build a home for the woman he hoped to marry. It was sad to see him go, but when he compounded that treachery by suing dear Mr. Ripley and the Community to get back the money he had invested in buying shares, I believe the action was not only insulting but almost criminal.

Now more and more people are thinking about leaving the Community to go back into the wicked world. Where are the idealists who joined with us to form a newer, better world? I thought that when the Reverend Hopewell visited the Farm and talked with Mr. Ripley, he would be a savior to bring strength to the community. You shared with me the secret that he planned to invest in the Community and that all our troubles would be over when he did. But that did not happen. He began to shilly-shally. I saw him talking to the pretty Mrs. Pretlove and I wondered whether her charms would outweigh the charms of the Community. I could see that he was wavering. When I looked at his face I could see weakness there and not the strength I had thought he possessed. He was a weak man, but he was our only hope as others slipped away. That was when I overheard a conversation between Charles Dana and your husband that suggested he too might be leaving. It was too much to bear.

I decided I would confront Mr. Hopewell and remind him of his promises and his duties. He has money to invest. He promised to support the Community. It would be evil for him to turn away—the work of the devil who is always trying to corrupt devout clergymen.

Every morning I am up early. I kneel at my window and pray for guidance and for the strength of our Community. When I saw the Reverend Hopewell walk over to the woods near the blueberry bog one morning, I decided to follow him and speak to him in the quiet of the morning. Perhaps the Lord would soften his heart. Before I could waver in my resolve, I dressed and went out.

It was not difficult to see him among the trees, although the sun had not yet risen. I seized a hoe from the barn to serve as a staff as I walked up the hill to meet him. He turned toward me expectantly and I realized he had been waiting for someone else. His expression dimmed when he saw it was only me—a reaction I am well used to seeing, but he was as always, the gentleman.

"You are out very early this morning, Miss Gray. Have you come to cultivate some plants up here?" he asked looking at my hoe.

I quickly disabused him of the notion that my mind was on plants as I told him of my disappointment in his reluctance to invest in our Community as he had promised. He told me a story about having to redeem a debt his father was unjustly collecting and how this good deed left him embarrassed for ready money. I must have looked askance at this tale, because he quickly tried to bolster it.

"I truly am embarrassed, Miss Gray. I am not a wealthy man and do not always have funds available to support every worthy cause. Do not look at me that way. I admire your Community, but as I explained to George Ripley, I shall have to postpone any investment for several more months or perhaps a year."

I am afraid that my anger overwhelmed me then. I could think of nothing except that he had told me he was giving us no money at all. This at a time when so many others had disappointed us. I raised the hoe and shook it at him as I said something—I cannot remember what it was, but I think I was shouting—and I saw a shocked look on his face. He never expected such words from me. No one ever expects me to raise my voice or have views of my own. No one ever listens to me, so why should Reverend Hopewell?

Before I thought about it I had raised the hoe and struck out at him. I could not help myself. It was as if my arm acted all on its own. A red gash appeared on his forehead and then he fell. I did not expect him to fall and I almost raised my voice again to demand that he stand up and talk to me. But he was lying very still. He must have hit his head on one of the rocks strewn about the wooded area. He groaned and reached out one arm for a moment, but it fell to the ground and after that he did not move.

I do not remember exactly what happened after that. I stood for a while then heard a noise and turned to see Abigail Pretlove in her white dress climbing up the hill toward us. I slipped behind the bushes that grow along the edge of the wood. A minute later Abigail was screaming. That shocked me to my senses and I went to her to comfort her, but by this time Mrs. Geary was running up the hill and Fred too. We all clustered around Abigail and tried to comfort her.

Soon there was a crowd. Someone led Abigail away and the others stood staring down at Winslow Hopewell, I among them. There were many suggestions as to what had happened and the men vied with each other to explain the story. I said not a word. No one would have heard me. No one ever listens to me. No one ever has.

You know what happened after that. The crowds, the arguments. The reporter, who seems still to be here at the Farm. I have no one to talk to. No one to whom I can explain what happened and I cannot live with the suspicions and fear here. I am leaving this very day to go see Reverend Carter at the Dedham Church. He and his wife will be a comfort in time of need. He has been doing God's work in rescuing runaway Africans trying to get to

Canada. Perhaps I can help in his work. There is no future at Brook Farm. The world we dreamed of will never come.

Farewell, dear Sophia. You were my only friend in school and through the long years afterwards. You are the only person I regret leaving. I hoped so much to build a new home here, but there is no home for me except perhaps someday a home in Heaven. God Bless you and your husband in all your endeavors.

Your loving friend,

Fanny Gray

Fanny left the letter on her writing table for Sophia to find in the morning and prepared to leave. The sky was growing dark, but the sun had not yet set and there was a sparkle on the snow-covered lawn from the sinking sun. She pulled on her stoutest pair of boots and buttoned them securely then pulled out her warmest mittens and scarf, the ones she had knitted during her first winter here. She loved the cheerful bright red color. The future had looked bright and cheerful when she started knitting them. Her warm gray cloak was more somber, more in tune with her thoughts as she closed the door and started across the back pasture.

With luck she could reach Dedham in less than two hours, but even then it would be completely dark, so she took a small lantern from the storeroom at the barn and lit it before leaving. She could see light in the kitchen, a flickering light from the fireplace and the oil lamp on the kitchen table. The kitchen crew would be helping Mrs. Geary prepare dinner and setting the table for the meal. The sound of Fred's voice drifted across the field. He always loved to sing at his work and Ellen often joined in:

The world is all a fleeting show

For Man's illusion given;

The smiles of joy, the tears of woe

Deceitful shine, deceitful flow

There's nothing true but heaven!

Never truer words were said or spoken. Would she ever see heaven? Would God ever forgive her for the terrible thing she did? She had tried so hard to make the world better and instead she always seemed to make it worse. Was she a terrible sinner? She wondered about that dreamily as though she were thinking of someone else. Someone who might have thought of killing a man. Not Fanny Gray who always did as she was told and never caused trouble for anyone. God would be wrong to condemn her, but perhaps God makes mistakes too. What a dreadful thing to think! She pushed that thought out of her mind. She was always a good girl and God must know that and send some reward.

The snow was getting a little heavier as the light grew dimmer. The snow clouds hid the moon and stars. There was nothing but her little lantern in the whole dark world. Thank the Lord there was a snow cover and the whiteness made the ground look a bit lighter. The dark trees and bushes stood out against the white. She had to be careful to keep on the road and not wander off into a ditch. She should have waited until morning. She knew that. The road went right past Cow Island Pond. She could follow the edge of the pond around and then she would be very close to Dedham. But she mustn't fall in this snow.

Something flickered over to the right. She stared into the darkness trying to see whether there was anything there—nothing-- just blackness. Then a little flicker again. Was it the eyes of an animal reflecting the lantern light? Could it be another person? A snow flurry stung her checks and filled her eyes with spots blotting out everything. She blinked to melt them and peered into the darkness again. No, that was no animal. That must be a lantern. She called out. "Hello, helloooo. Is anyone there?" No answer.

She turned and started forward again. If anything the snow was heavier, stinging her cheeks, running down her forehead from her hair, and forcing her to close her eyes into narrow slits. Every step seemed to take longer.

Then there was a voice. "Hello? Hello anyone?" It was a woman's voice. Fanny stood still and peered around. The light was closer this time and she saw a dark figure holding it, a bulky figure bundled in a long skirt or cloak and very big on top. Finally she was only a few feet away and she could see it was a woman carrying a baby. What was she doing out here in the storm?

There was no time to ask questions. When the woman got quite close they peered at each other's faces. Fanny gasped as she realized it was the black face of the African runaway, Lily. "What are you doing here? Where is your husband?"

"He got caught. He must have. He went out and when he didn't come back and didn't come back, I knew I'd have to take the baby to Canada myself. You're Miz Gray that's a friend of Miz Whitelaw?"

"Yes, and I'm your friend too. We'd better walk together. I'll take you to Dedham and you can stay with Reverend Carter until the snow lets up. You can't walk far in this snow."

They moved on. It was a little better with two lanterns. Fanny could see more of the road, but the ditch was so filled with snow it looked just like road. One time she stepped in snow up to the top of her boot just where she thought the road would be. Snow was stinging her face and she worried about the baby. Lily had him wrapped in some sort of shawl, but it wasn't warm enough. Fanny pulled off her red scarf and wrapped it around him. Then the snow came creeping in around her collar and her neck and shoulders were cold. But she was strong and could survive a lot of snow and troubles too. A big, strong, strapping girl they used to call her.

Lily's head was bowed. She sobbed as she walked and muttered prayers under her breath. Fanny started singing a hymn and Lily joined in with a quiet, sweet voice:

Oh God our strength in ages past

Our rock upon the sea

Protect thy children now we ask

And let us come to thee.

The snow was getting deeper and it tangled their ankles and in some spots was above the tops of their boots making the skin raw under their stockings. Fanny's skirt was soaking wet and it got heavier and heavier and icy cold against her legs. How much further did they have to walk?

"Look," Lily cried. "There's a clear space with no trees. We can walk across there." She veered to the right and struck off past a few pine trees toward a large patch of clear snow. Why was it so clear? Why no bushes or undergrowth? Suddenly Fanny knew.

"No, Lily, that's the pond. Don't go there. The ice may not be strong enough." But the wind was blowing toward her and it blew the words away from Lily. She kept going, clutching the baby in her arms.

Fanny started after her, struggling to catch up. Lily was so small and light she was faster on the snowy ground. Fanny couldn't quite catch up.

"Stop, stop!" Fanny shouted, leaning so far toward her that she stumbled and fell into the snow. Up again she pressed on. Lily was past the last tree now and on the snowy pond. Fanny strained to hear any noise. And then it came—a groan as the ice started to give way. And then a sharp crack as it broke. Fanny was out on the pond now, racing toward Lily.

"Give me the baby! I have to save the baby! He mustn't die. He mustn't."

There was another loud crack and the pond suddenly opened up in front of her. Lily and the baby were sliding, sliding. Fanny reached toward them stretching her arms. Another sharp crack and then a widening path of dark black water...

CHAPTER TWENTY NINE

Charlotte Learns the Truth

November 20, 1842

After Fanny left the parlor, Daniel and Charlotte stared at each other. Minutes passed.

"What do we do now?" asked Daniel.

"Fanny must have been there," Charlotte answered. "She looked so guilty. She knows we've found out. How did it happen? We must tell Mr. Ripley about it. That's the first thing."

Charlotte usually found George Ripley an easy man to talk to. His face shone with kindness. But this was different. Charlotte dreaded telling him about Fanny. What if he didn't believe her? How could she accuse his wife's best friend of killing someone?

Her stomach hurt and she wanted to rush back to her room, throw herself on the bed and pull the blanket over her head. This was like the moment when her ship pulled out of the harbor at Southampton and she left her whole life behind. But it had to be done. She looked out the window, the sun had disappeared and the snow was getting heavier.

222 | ADELE FASICK

"You had better go back to Boston" she told Daniel. "It may take a while to find Mr. Ripley and speak to him privately. This is something I have to do myself."

"Yes, he won't want an outsider like me to be in on the conversation." Daniel stopped talking and looked at her with a frown, "I'd rather stay, but I'd better go back to my boarding house now. I'll come out tomorrow to see how that talk went."

Daniel left and Charlotte cast a worried look at the sky hoping the snow wouldn't be worse tomorrow. What if a real storm blew up and they were snowbound, cooped up in the house with a secret so big it was weighing on her every minute? It would be like being trapped inside a barn with a wild horse, or a rampaging bull. Not that Fanny was anything like a raging bull, but she must have gone mad to have done something like this and there was no telling what a mad woman might do.

When Charlotte knocked at the door of George Ripley's study and was told to come in, she found him at his desk bent over a large ledger. He looked up and pushed his glasses up on his forehead before he spoke.

"What is it, Charlotte?" He rubbed his forehead as if he wanted to clear his mind. "You look perturbed. Is anything wrong? Did one of the children misbehave during lessons today? Sit down and tell me about it." His smile was genial, but it didn't erase the worry in his eyes. Did he really think he would be able to wipe away her troubles with a kind word or two?

"I wish it were only the children misbehaving, but I'm afraid it is much more serious. It's hard to say this." Charlotte paused and sighed then started again. "I am afraid that the person who killed

Reverend Hopewell is one of our members. It's dreadful, but...but I to have to tell you about it."

Mr. Ripley's smile disappeared. He slammed the ledger closed and gave Charlotte his full attention while she told him what she and Daniel had discovered. He knew nothing about the days they had spent tracking down all the people who might have been responsible.

"We thought for a while that Mr. Platt's brother Roger might have been angry at Reverend Hopewell. But we discovered that Winslow Hopewell had paid off Roger Platt's debt to his father. He would have been grateful, not angry.

"Then we investigated Mr. Whitelaw, whose wife had been very fond of Reverend Hopewell. But eventually we learned that he was in New York at the time.

"The person who was always close by was Fanny Gray. She had been at the Farm. She was at the scene immediately after Reverend Hopewell was discovered. And the more people we questioned, the more often someone mentioned that a woman had been seen in the woods earlier that morning. Tonight when I asked her about whether she was there, Fanny was frightened and ran out of the room."

By this time Mr. Ripley had gotten up from his chair. He was standing very still with his back toward Charlotte looking out the window at the darkening sky and falling snow. When she had finished he turned to her.

"I don't know what to say, or to think. We must talk with Fanny. Oh, poor Sophia, how she will suffer to hear that a lifelong friend has come to this!"

They were interrupted by the sound of the supper bell, so he added, "We will speak about this more after supper. Please do not mention it to anyone else, but of course you would not do that."

Supper was a dismal meal. Charlotte could scarcely eat anything. Fred teased her, saying "Are you dreaming of good British beefsteak, Charlotte, and scorning our New England baked beans?" She knew he was joking, but it hurt her face to smile back at him. She looked around the tables for Fanny, but could not see her anywhere. She was probably lurking in the kitchen, too embarrassed to come into the dining hall. After the final grace, the Ripleys stood up and left the room. George Ripley glanced back and shook his head. Charlotte knew he was going to tell Sophia the dreadful news.

Time passed slowly. When the kitchen was cleared and there were no tasks for her to bury herself in, Charlotte went into the parlor and sat in a corner. John Dwight was playing the piano and a group of students sat on the floor listening to the soothing strains. Lamps flickered on the side tables and a fire burned cheerily in the fireplace. Everything was peaceful except Charlotte's mind. She jumped every time she heard a footstep. Finally Sophia Ripley glided in and without saying a word, tapped her on the shoulder and beckoned her. They went to George Ripley's study.

Sophia looked pale as she explained. "When I heard the news, it took me a while to understand what had happened." She clutched a handkerchief in her hand and touched it briefly to her eyes.

"I had to speak to Fanny and I knew she had not come to supper. I went to her room and knocked on the door. There was no answer to all my knocking, so I finally opened the door and went in. The room was empty and cold, but Fanny had left a note on the table for me. Here it is."

She handed Fanny's note to Charlotte who read it slowly and carefully. By the time she was finished she was unable to hold back her tears. Sophia reached toward her and patted her shoulder.

"What shall we do?" Charlotte cried. The thought of going to the sheriff was almost unbearable.

"Tomorrow morning, Charlotte, you and I will go to see the Reverend Carter in Dedham," Sophia answered. "Perhaps Fanny will be willing to talk with us and we can think about what can be done."

The next morning the sun was out and the clouds had all but disappeared. Charlotte could hear the drip of melting snow falling from the eaves as the sun warmed it. Streaks of frost on the window dimmed the sunlight, but it too was melting, turning into drops of water sliding down the pane as though even the house was weeping. Ellen must have gone downstairs early to help in the kitchen, but Charlotte hated the thought of getting out of bed and facing the day. Finally she climbed out, dressed and splashed her face with the icy water from the water pitcher.

There was enough snow on the road so Mrs. Ripley and Charlotte could take the sleigh to drive to Dedham. The trip didn't take long and they were warmly welcomed by Reverend Carter and his wife, Sarah, who were astonished to see them so early in the morning. Charlotte saw no sign of Fanny and when they asked about her, the Carters looked at one another in surprise.

Sarah Carter turned to Sophia and said, "Fanny Gray did not come here yesterday. We haven't seen her now in several weeks, although she often comes to Sunday services. We thought the bad weather must have kept her away."

"But she left a note saying she was coming here," Charlotte insisted. "Where could she have gone if she did not come here?"

"Have you asked any of your neighbors? Perhaps she decided Dedham was too far to travel in the snow." suggested John Carter.

"That might be true," said Sophia bravely. "We'll certainly inquire. I am sorry we bothered you. It is very early in the day for calls, but we have been rather worried about Fanny. If she should arrive, would you please send someone over to let us know?"

The Carters promised they would help as much as they could and sent them on their way with smiles and assurances that the Lord would certainly watch over such a godly woman as Fanny. Charlotte did not find those words reassuring. The horse was eager to get back to the barn so the trip home was even faster than the one over, but it was much gloomier.

"What could have happened? What could have happened?" Sophia repeated several times

"I have no idea," Charlotte answered, although she had a horrible vision of Fanny losing her way as the darkness came and perhaps falling in the snow and freezing. She didn't want to think about that. Perhaps Fanny had gone somewhere else. Perhaps she had found someone who would drive her to Boston. She could have gone to see her friend Tabitha Whitelaw. Tabitha would have taken care of her. Charlotte was sure of that.

They drove the sleigh into the barnyard and unhitched the horse. Several men and boys were in the barn mending harnesses under the direction of Mr. Platt. When they heard the story, everyone tried to figure out what might have happened.

"She might have walked into the Cow Island Pond," said Mr. Platt gloomily. "That road runs right by there and it's easy to miss your way in the dark."

"No, that's not possible," gasped Sophia. "I will speak to Mr. Ripley and see what he suggests." She moved quickly toward the house, while Charlotte lingered behind.

"Perhaps we should walk over to the Pond," she said quietly to Mr. Platt. We must find out what happened."

Neither of them said anything as they made their way along the soggy road. Snow was melting from the center, but it lingered in the ditches and in shaded places under the trees. Sparrows twittered in the branches of the pines and tiny nuthatches crept up and down the trunks trying to find something to eat. Loud cawing of crows made Charlotte shiver. What had they discovered on the snowy fields? Only a dead rabbit or two she hoped.

At the place where the road curved to the left toward Dedham, Mr. Platt veered to the right, although it was impossible to see the pond. In summer the blue water was visible through the trees, but everything was white today. They crunched through the snow toward the bare white expanse that was the pond. Mr. Platt walked ahead, clearing a path of sorts and Charlotte tried to follow in his footprints. Then she heard his voice raised in a harsh cry.

"God Almighty! Look at this!"

Charlotte's heart pounded and she felt dizzy as she caught up to him to see what he was looking at. There it was half-buried in the snow, a black leather satchel. Maybe it's not Fanny's she thought desperately, and pulled at it to free it from the snow. There they were—clearly visible on the leather tab—the initials F.L.G. Frances Lucinda Gray. It was Fanny's satchel.

Mr. Platt cleared his throat and spat into the snow. He wasn't a man to show his feelings, but there was sadness in his face. "Fanny Gray was a fine strong woman," he muttered. "She helped my Hetty with the pigs one time when they got out of their pen. She helped." He cleared his throat again and picked up the bag. "I'll get some of the men together and we can walk around the pond and see what we can find."

They turned to retrace their steps back to the Farm. The clouds were starting to cover the sun and the wind was picking up. Even the birds had fallen silent and retreated to their nests. It might be a long time before they found anything more.

CHAPTER THIRTY

Charlotte Looks Back

November 1, 1843. – One Year Later

Dried leaves were scuttling across the brown lawn—dead, dying. Charlotte hated November. It reminded her of that dreadful day at Cow Island Pond more than a year ago. She had been in a haze for the rest of the day after they found Fanny's satchel. George Ripley and most of the men and boys went back to the pond with Abner Platt to search around the edges. They found a body caught in the rushes along the edge of the water, but it wasn't Fanny. It was a black African woman clutching a baby in her arms. Her arms were so tight around the baby they couldn't pry him out; the elbows wouldn't bend. So they were buried together in one coffin. It was probably the most respectful way.

It wasn't until two days later when the ice was half gone from the pond that the men found Fanny. The freezing water had preserved her body perfectly. People said she looked exactly the same as she had when she was alive. Charlotte thought she looked younger, even happier somehow. She looked peaceful. Had Fanny ever felt so peaceful before?

The sheriff came out to the Farm of course and talked to the Ripleys and to Charlotte. Sophia showed him the letter Fanny had left and Charlotte tried to tell him about what she and Daniel had been doing. How they had tried to discover what had happened and how the search had finally led to Fanny. He wanted to talk to Daniel too, and when the inquest came, the Ripleys and Daniel and Charlotte all gave testimony. The final verdict was that it was "death by misadventure" for Fanny and for Lily Lawrence and her baby. The judge said he saw no reason for changing the verdict on Winslow Hopewell's death. That too remained "death by misadventure". That was really what it was.

"Misadventure"—what a strange word. When Charlotte was young she had thought adventures were glorious. She had visions of knights in shining armor mounted on milk white steeds or discoverers sailing across the ocean to find new lands. Adventures in storybooks never go awry. Foolish accidents like wandering into a frozen pond in the snow or meeting an angry woman with a hoe don't appear in storybooks.

A memorial service was held at Brook Farm for Fanny and for Lily. Two of Fanny's brothers were there. One of them said a few, more than a few, eloquent words about how much he and his brothers had appreciated the loving care Fanny had taken of them after their mother died. He spoke so well that Charlotte thought Fanny must have been wrong about none of them paying any attention to her. Then Tabitha Whitelaw spoke about how hard Fanny had worked to save runaway African slaves. She also talked about Lily Lawrence and her husband and how they had struggled to reach the freedom they longed for.

After the service, the brothers took Fanny's coffin back to Port Augusta to be buried in their family plot. The Reverend John Carter took the coffin holding Lily and her baby back to the Dedham Church and gave them a decent burial. Abigail and Charlotte, as well as several other people from Brook Farm, walked over to Dedham to see them laid to rest.

On the morning of that funeral the sun was shining and the snow had almost disappeared, making the day seem more like early spring than the beginning of winter. They walked along the muddy road, not saying much until Abigail startled Charlotte by asking, "Do you think I ought to tell Thomas Hopewell that he has a grandson?"

Charlotte drew her breath in surprise. That had never occurred to her, although once it was said, the idea seemed natural. She thought of Thomas Hopewell sitting alone in his grand house night after night. Sophia Ripley had told Charlotte she and her husband had visited the Reverend Thomas Hopewell and he found it consoling that the death of his son was almost accidental and not the result of any vicious criminal. Charlotte wasn't sure she would find much consolation in that, but it seemed to help the Reverend Hopewell. Wouldn't he be glad to know that some spark of his son remained? Why shouldn't Abigail and Timothy go to live with him and carry on the family name? But what if he still rejected Quakers? What if he rejected Abigail and only wanted Timothy?

"That's a big question, Abigail," she finally answered. "Is that what you want to do? Do you think it would be best for Timothy?"

Abigail pulled her cloak tighter around her shoulders and walked along silently for a few minutes. "I don't know. I just don't know," she muttered. "Does Timothy have a right to know the truth? We talked about that, Winslow and I, on the last day I saw him. He said he could persuade his father to recognize our marriage and he said we could have another wedding—a "real" wedding—and everything would be all right. But I think he expected that I would stop being a Quaker and join his church. I'm not sure I want that. I don't believe Timothy should grow up to believe in war, maybe to go to war."

"America won't go to war, Abigail," Charlotte assured her. "We've won our independence and we have a country far away from Europe and all its wars. You don't have to worry about that. Think how happy Reverend Hopewell would be to find out he has a grand-son."

"Would he be happy? Well, he'd be happy about Timothy, I'm sure. Who wouldn't be happy to have such a fine boy? But would he accept me? Would he just snatch Timothy away and make him his own? He is Winslow's father, but he is also a selfish old man. He only loves people who do just as he says." Her steps grew quicker and her skirts swung around her as she walked so briskly Charlotte had to hurry to keep up. She was frowning now as though she were looking Thomas Hopewell in the eye and not liking what she found. Then she stopped abruptly. "I will wait on it," she said. "I will wait for the spirit to speak to my condition. Then I will know what is right to do."

The next few weeks were odd. Everyone went about their usual activities, but it felt as though they were walking on eggshells, tip-toeing so as not to upset anyone. People took care to be nice to one another. Fred and the other students organized a concert for New Year's Day and everyone sang hymns and listened to readings by members and guests. Margaret Fuller was there and when her turn came she read a poem by Ralph Waldo Emerson about berrying. Had Mr. Emerson thought of Brook Farm when he wrote it? One thing they did well was to pick berries and make use of the blueberries, blackberries and raspberries found in the woods around the Farm. It had been one of Fanny's special pleasures. Was that why the poem was chosen?

Berrying

"May be true what I had heard,
Earth's a howling wilderness
Truculent with fraud and force,"
Said I, strolling through the pastures,
And along the riverside.
Caught among the blackberry vines,
Feeding on the Ethiops sweet,
Pleasant fancies overtook me:
I said, "What influence me preferred
Elect to dreams thus beautiful?"
The vines replied, "And didst thou deem
No wisdom to our berries went?"

Winter is always a somber time in Massachusetts, but at least they weren't isolated on some rural farm when the snow came and kept everyone indoors. Charlotte continued teaching the children as they grew and learned. She was pleased by the way the small ones who had known none of their letters when they started in the autumn had learned them all by the time January came. Timothy of course learned everything very quickly and was reading Aesop's fables by himself, but even little Johnny Parsons was able to get through the shorter ones without many stumbles.

Almost every Sunday all through that long winter Daniel managed to get out to the Farm. He and Charlotte spent hours in the parlor talking about his job and his plans. His article about Winslow

Hopewell's death had impressed Mr. Cabot, so he now worked regularly for the *Evening Transcript*. When he was first taken on the staff she teased him by asking how an "ignorant immigrant" could write about the ins-and-outs of Boston, but after a few months he knew more about Boston than she did despite her three years head start on living in the city. Then it was his turn to call her an "ignorant immigrant". Sophia Ripley was shocked one afternoon when she overheard him say that, but to Daniel and Charlotte it was a badge of honor to have learned so much about their new country and to feel at home in it.

Spring finally came. The bite went out of the wind and once again it was a pleasure to walk through the woods. Daniel and Charlotte walked over to Cow Island Pond one afternoon in March and stood at the edge thinking about Fanny, and about Lily too, and of the way lives could be snuffed out so quickly.

Everything was different than it had been in the fall. There were fewer people at the Farm. Leaves were coming out on the trees around the pond, but Charlotte wondered how the crops would do with fewer people to plant and harvest them. Fanny had wanted so much for the Community to survive, but even she had not survived the long cold winter.

Daniel was still looking at the gray-blue water of the pond. "I am going to write a poem about all this," he said. "Then I will have it to remember when I leave."

Leave? The word cut into Charlotte's mind. He had not mentioned leaving. He looked at her and she could see worry in his eyes. "Horace Greeley has asked me to go to New York City and work for his new newspaper *The Tribune*," he said. "I can't miss this chance. Have you ever thought of leaving?"

No, she had not thought of such a thing. But as he talked she started thinking. So many people were going. Mr. Ripley was talking about turning the Community into a Phalanx—a very different kind of place where people were organized into rigid groups and each group had its task. Charlotte wasn't sure she would like a community like that. She hesitated and Daniel spoke again.

"We could go to New York together, two ignorant immigrants in a new city. My pay will be better there and I've been saving money every week since I started working for Mr. Cabot."

"That money was so you could send for your mother and sisters," Charlotte reminded him. "Anyway, I don't need your pay. I have been taking care of myself for ever since I left home. If I go to New York, I'll pay my own way."

They left it at that and walked back to the Hive. A few days after Easter, Daniel left for New York. He loved his work with the *New York Tribune* and wrote letters every week about what he was doing in the city. He went to plays and to concerts. He even heard the famous violinist, Ole Bull, at his first concert in America. Ellen teased Charlotte about all the letters. She claimed Jonas Gerritson was growing weary dragging all the mail up to the Farm and his horse was wearing out. She also said that for all the money Charlotte spent on postage she could live for a year in New York and not have to write letters.

Abigail had not yet decided whether to tell Thomas Hopewell the truth about Timothy, who was growing and learning every day. He was a happy boy and Abigail and Charlotte agreed he would grow up to be a great man. Abigail wanted him to become the patriot who would finally end slavery in America. She and Tabitha Whitelaw had been working hard to prepare the ground for that change.

Sometimes Charlotte could see traces of sadness about Abigail, perhaps when she thought of lost plans and dreams, but most of the time she was serene, moving around the house in her white dress like a beautiful statue come to life. Charlotte believed that the spirit, whatever she meant by that, had spoken to her condition and she was at peace.

So many people were moving and changing. Margaret Fuller had gone to New York to work for Horace Greeley's newspaper, just as Daniel was. She wrote often to Sophia Ripley and early in October she had sent a letter to Charlotte. In her letter, Miss Fuller described a new school opening in the city to teach the children of the Free Blacks in the city. The director of the school was looking for teachers who would be willing to teach the young children. Miss Fuller urged Charlotte to apply.

Charlotte wrote to tell Daniel about Miss Fuller's suggestion and he responded enthusiastically. He said that despite how much he enjoyed his job, he found himself often alone in New York and missed having her to talk to. He even sent her one of his poems:

Sad the bird that sings alone,

Flies to wilds, unseen to languish,

Pours, unheard, the ceaseless moan,

And wastes on desert air its anguish!

Charlotte smiled to think he was becoming so poetical, but she carried that little poem with her everywhere and read it over whenever she was alone. Another winter was arriving, but she could hope that this year the season would bring new lives for them instead of sorrow.

The Death of a Dream: After Brook Farm

Weep not that the world changes -- did it keep a stable, changeless state, it were cause indeed to weep. –William Cullen Bryant "Mutation"

The Brook Farm experiment lasted less than seven years. George Ripley struggled with constant financial problems. Farming was not practical because the distance to markets made it impossible to sell enough produce. Although the school was very successful, other industries faltered because too few experienced working people were attracted to the community. Eventually Ripley tried to transform the community into a Phalanx, a rigid social group program in which people were assigned to work at specific tasks. The young, idiosyncratic rebels who had been the original members gradually drifted away. Several later became important figures in 19th century American society. And for most of them the Brook Farm experience was an important defining experience in their lives. Several later published memoirs of the community, but George Ripley never recorded his account of the experience.

George and Sophia Ripley moved to New York in 1847 where George Ripley joined the staff of Horace Greeley's newspaper the *New York Tribune*. He remained there for the rest of his career, usually as book editor, and died in 1880. Sophia converted to Catholicism soon after the couple moved to New York, but her life was cut short by breast cancer and she died in 1857.

Lydia Maria Child continued to write and lecture throughout her long life. In both fiction and nonfiction she supported the abolitionist movement and protested the mistreatment of American Indians by settlers and the government. She died in 1880.

Elizabeth Peabody maintained her influential bookstore in Boston until 1852. Later she became interested in German educational theories and in 1860 opened the first kindergarten in North America. Her writings on education inspired generations of American teachers. She died in 1894.

Margaret Fuller's best-known book, *Women in the Nineteenth Century*, was one of the foundations of the feminist movement and inspired leaders including Susan B. Anthony and Elizabeth Cady Stanton. She became a journalist and foreign correspondent for the *New York Tribune*, but her career was cut short by her death in a shipwreck at the age of 40 in 1850.

Bronson Alcott, perhaps best remembered as the father of Louisa May Alcott, was also an educator, a lecturer, and writer. He founded a short-lived communal group, Fruitlands, which espoused a more radical lifestyle than Brook Farm, including a vegan diet and a ban on using farm animals for labor. In later years he continued to give lectures and write about his philosophical theories. He died in 1888.

Charles Dana, like Ripley, moved to New York and worked for Horace Greeley. He served as a foreign correspondent for the *New York Tribune* in Europe. During the Civil War he was appointed Assistant Secretary of War. Later he bought the *New York Sun* and built it into an important newspaper. He died in 1897.

John Sullivan Dwight lived in New England all of his life. His marriage to Mary Bullard, another Brook Farmer, was a happy one, but unfortunately she died young and he never remarried. As the founder and editor of *Dwight's Journal of Music* he became the foremost American music critic of the nineteenth century. He died in 1893.

Nathaniel Hawthorne lived briefly at Brook Farm but found the commitment to farm labor was not compatible with his desire to write nor with his desire to marry Sophia Peabody (Elizabeth Peabody's sister). Eventually he sued the community in a vain attempt to get back some of the money he had invested in the project. Hawthorne's novel *The Blithedale Romance* is said to be based in part on his memories of Brook Farm.

Sources of Quotations

Page

2 "There's Nothing True But Heaven" (1829) From Thomas Moore's *Sacred Songs.* This was a favorite hymn sung at Brook Farm.

17 "The Barrow Girl" from Collection of ballads, songsheets. 2 vols. London: J. Pitts, 1805-1840

49 Wit and Wisdom of the Rev. Sydney Smith by Sydney Smith p. 70 (Google books)

56 "A Nation Once Again" An Irish Rebel Song, written By Thomas Davis.

68 "Ode to Autumn" by John Keats

77 "Must not a woman be..." by John Keats "Ode to Fanny"

101 "We'll drink to-night with hearts as light", by Charles Fenno Hoffman "O Fleeting Love"

121 "Cape Cod Girls" http://shanty.rendance.org/lyrics/showlyric.php/capecod

233 "Berrying" by Ralph Waldo Emerson

236 An old Irish lament translated into English by Charlotte Brooke in *Reliques of Irish Poetry* (1789)

Other Books about Brook Farm and its Friends

Baker, Carlos. *Emerson Among the Eccentrics: A Group Portrait.* New York: Viking Press, 1996.

Codman, John Thomas. *Brook Farm; Historic and Personal Memoirs.* Boston: Arena publishing company, 1894.

Curtis, Edith Roelker. *A Season in Utopia; the Story of Brook Farm.* New York,: Nelson, 1961.

Delano, Sterling F. *Brook Farm : The Dark Side of Utopia.* Cambridge, Mass.: Belknap Press of Harvard University Press, 2004.

Fasick, Adele. *Margaret Fuller: An Uncommon Woman.* San Francisco. MonganBooks, 2012.

Karcher, Carolyn L. *The First Woman in the Republic: A Cultural Biography of Lydia Maria Child.* New Americanists. Durham: Duke University Press, 1994.

Orvis, Marianne. *Letters from Brook Farm, 1844-1847.* The American Utopian Adventure. Philadelphia,: Porcupine Press, 1972.

Swift, Lindsay. *Brook Farm.* New York: The Macmillan Company, 1900.

Made in the USA
Charleston, SC
05 May 2014